MY MASTER MARINER

My Master Mariner

by
Judith Saxton

Dales Large Print Books
Long Preston, North Yorkshire,
England.

British Library Cataloguing in Publication Data.

Saxton, Judith
My Master Mariner.

A catalogue record for this book is
available from the British Library

ISBN 1-85389-884-8 pbk

First published in Great Britain by Robert Hale & Co.,
Ltd., 1974

Dales Large Print is an imprint of
Library Magna Books Ltd.
Printed and bound in Great Britain by
T.J. International Ltd., Cornwall, PL28 8RW.

For Monica and Derrick,
'Where our caravan has rested'!

Spain is a country of long memories. I, who am writing this book, was cruising in the Mediterranean as an officer under Admiral Sir Reginald Hall of the Naval Intelligence Division; and I could not but be aware of a special unfriendliness shown in many quiet ways by the Governor of Cadiz. In the end he was asked with the due courtesies, why. The Governor received the question with profound astonishment that anything so inevitable should not have been understood: and he exclaimed with an incredulity which his good manners could not quite conceal, 'Have you forgotten Drake?'

A.E.W. Mason, *The Life of Francis Drake*

(Reproduced by kind permission of Trinity College, Oxford, and Hodder & Stoughton Ltd.)

ACKNOWLEDGEMENTS

I should like to express my thanks to the Librarian and staff of the Plymouth City Library, and to the staff of the Wrexham Public Library, all of whom gave me valuable help.

J.T.

1

ESCAPE FROM COMBE SYDENHAM

'I imagine, my dear Eliza, that you might well be pleased to hear that you are to attend the Queen at Court. But is it dutiful—is it *polite*—to display such an excess of pleasure?'

Lady Elizabeth Sydenham looked sternly at her daughter, who dutifully tried to stifle her delight at the prospect of leaving Sydenham Castle, where she had spent the first fourteen years of her life.

'My pleasure is not at the thought of leaving you, or my father,' the girl said obediently, 'but I've heard so much about the delights of Queen Elizabeth's Court, the beauties of the palaces and the sights of the city of London. And I long to meet girls of my own age—and young men as well.'

She said the last words rather defiantly.

As the only child of elderly parents, she had grown used to being treated as though

13

she were as delicate as porcelain in some ways, and with unnecessary severity in others. She had been brought up to know her worth, and she had also been brought up in the unconscious attitude of the only child—*she* often felt far more responsible for her parents than they did for her. But she suffered most from having no friends of her own age. Even the local girls were debarred from her as companions, in case they became too familiar, or taught Eliza bad habits. Her maid, Isabelle, was her only *confidante*, and the closeness of their relationship had to be hidden from Sir George and his wife, who would have thought it highly improper for their child to ignore her position in life, and indulge in gossip with a servant.

But, to Elizabeth's relief, the words 'young men' brought no sharp word of restraint from her mother's thin, painted lips. Quite the opposite, in fact.

'Exactly, my child. Oh, I know in the past you have thought us unnatural parents, to have kept you close to us, allowing you very little freedom to meet other young people. But Sir George has always had it in mind that you should go to Court. There you will meet the cream of the nobility.

14

You will have a wideness of choice in your search for a marriage partner that we could never have offered you here.'

'Yes, I do understand, Mother. Will I be able to take Isabelle with me?'

'Of course, Eliza. Isabelle has been your personal maid for two years now. Upon her will rest the care and responsibility for your clothes. And you will take a manservant—Hal from the stable—who can bring messages home, and will look after your horses at Court, and see that you're well mounted for every occasion.'

'Did it take my father long to persuade the Queen to allow me to serve her?'

Elizabeth's mother looked wary. 'You are young, of course. But your education has been good, and you can sew and keep house well enough. I dare say you'll manage to please her Majesty.'

Elizabeth stifled an impatient exclamation and bent her head over the embroidery on her lap. The room was warm enough, for a big fire blazed on the hearth, and the bowls of early daffodils had already burst from the confines of bud into golden bloom. But draughts crept insidiously into the big chamber, stirring the rushes on the floor and making the long tapestries sway

15

against the stone walls. Both women had embroidered firescreens to protect their complexions from the heat, and Elizabeth kept hers conscientiously between her face and the flames, for she knew what havoc heat could wreak on her delicate skin.

Now, as she embroidered a partlet with neat, swift stitches, she thought remorsefully that it had been selfish and thoughtless to show her delight at the thought of leaving home. After all, the careful guarding of their daughter from the company of any but her tutor might mean that she was inexperienced, but the time she grudged at her lessons, and bustling round the castle behind her mother, had been well spent. She had received an education that fitted her for the Court, young though she was. Her tutor was a charming and able man. Her languages were good, she spoke French and Italian with an impeccable accent and her grasp of Latin was sufficient for most purposes. She was an avid reader, and modern writers, particularly the poets, delighted her. She had been taught to ride a horse well and with grace, to shoot with the long bow, to hunt and to hawk. Perhaps, after all, her time had been better spent in such pastimes than in gossiping with other girls, or eyeing young men.

'Many of the courtiers are poets, are they not?' she ventured after a moment. 'I might meet Spenser, Gascoigne, Philip Sidney even. Why, I might see Francis Drake, who has just sailed round the world and brought the Queen a fabulous treasure!'

'Perhaps. Though Drake is a commoner, he is a good Devonshire man. Though no one knows yet whether the Queen will treat him as a hero or a common corsair,' Lady Elizabeth said serenely. 'But remember, we are sending you to Court to become a lady, not to dream like some dairymaid of love and poetry. Your looks are—passable. You should please the Queen and, later on, others also.'

Elizabeth lapsed into a dream of the glory to come. She was beautiful, her mirror told her that. Thick dark hair with a natural curl, big brown eyes fringed with black lashes, a three-cornered smile that brought a dimple to her cheek. She would be well dressed, trust Lady Elizabeth for that, and though she was slim and pale skinned, she was also healthy and strong. She looked down at her hands holding the embroidery and a smile curved her mouth. My hands are like the Queen's, she thought. Slender fingers tipped with almond-shaped nails. I shall wear jewelled rings to draw attention to their whiteness when mother is not at hand to disapprove.

Her mother's voice brought her out of her reverie.

'Go to your room now, my dear, and change your dress. Your father is bringing some friends home for dinner.'

Elizabeth danced up the shallow stairs, calling for Isabelle and hearing that maiden's light and obedient footfalls as she hurried up the stairs after her mistress.

'We *are* to go to Court,' Elizabeth said triumphantly as the maid helped her into her best dress of orange-tawny velvet. 'That's why Mother has been so busy refurbishing my wardrobe with all those beautiful dresses and kirtles, sleeves and partlets. Hal from the stable is to come as well, to look after our horses and act as messenger, if need be.' She clasped her hands dramatically together. 'I've *dreamed* of this moment,' she assured her maid fervently.

'You'll have all the young men at your feet, Mistress,' said Isabelle, placing a

18

wreath of orange gilliflowers on Elizabeth's shining hair.

And Elizabeth, smiling at her reflection in the polished metal mirror, had to nod her agreement. She was sure she would love everyone at Court, and they would all love her.

2

THE LITTLE SYDENHAM

'Sydenham! Come, hurry, girl. Being young and small is no excuse now—the opposite, I should think, for you're almost small enough to wriggle into my jewelbox to find the ruby ring. Oh, bring me the box, for pity's sake, it would be quicker to find it myself.'

Elizabeth knew better than to obey a command like that. She scrabbled frantically in the huge box, discovered—more by luck than judgement—the ring she wanted, and hurried across to the Queen, the jewel in her hand but humiliation in her heart.

If I had dreamed it would be like this, she thought, as she put the ring carefully on the long finger already heavy with jewels which was jabbing furiously in her direction. She had been in the Queen's service as a maid of honour for almost a month, and she had never been unhappier nor worked so hard.

The other girls who worked, ate and played when she did, were almost all older than the little Sydenham. But, more important, they knew each other. Their families were intimate, and the Queen, though she spoke sharply to them also, was far easier with them than she was with Elizabeth.

'Poor Sydenham, in hot water again?'

The round, pretty face and sharp, sparkling eyes of Dorothy Howard were at Elizabeth's shoulder. Her words held malice, certainly, but a certain fellow feeling into the bargain. The Queen had no love for any of the Howard girls, who were renowned both for their loose morals and sexual appetites.

'No more than usual,' Elizabeth muttered. 'Why is her Majesty so especially sharp today? She seems excited one moment, and furious the next.'

'Goodness, Sydenham, you country girls! Don't you ever listen to gossip? You know the great treasure that Francis Drake brought back from his voyage round the world? Well, the Queen wants her share, naturally. She'll have it, too, no matter what. Why, a portion of the booty has

21

already been lodged in the Tower, and today Pirate Drake is coming to Court, to explain the—er—accident of his coming into possession of Spanish plate and jewels, to say nothing of holy relics.'

'Shall we see him? I would love to. He's talked about a lot in the West Country, and well loved. He must be a wonderful man.'

'Shouldn't think so, Sydenham. A quick glimpse, maybe. But he is to have a private audience with the Queen whilst they cook up some story for the Spanish Ambassador. It will have to be one that Philip of Spain can swallow, too, for the Queen doesn't want war,' she giggled, 'only treasure.'

'Why should the Queen have to invent a story for Mendoza, Dorothy? He's nothing but a strutting, self-important little cockerel.'

Another girl paused to listen to the question, and then said softly, 'Well, you've been at Court for nearly three weeks and you don't know *that!* Sydenham, you Somerset girls have heads as soft as boiled apples. Drake took Spanish treasure and raided Spanish territory—or so the Spaniards claim. But we *shall* see the great man, for the Queen gives her private audience to our pet pirate in an hour, and we are to accompany her to the great chamber.'

'But not inside it, Mary,' Dorothy whispered mournfully. 'Lord, I'd give my new pearl-and-gold necklace to be a fly on the wall in there whilst the Queen talks to her corsair—and Mendoza would probably give half his master's kingdom for the same privilege.'

'Shall we go, then, Mary?' asked Dorothy Howard. 'Her Majesty is ready.'

Mary Wriothesley nodded and smiled, taking Dorothy's hand, and the two left the room in the wake of the Queen, leaving Elizabeth Sydenham to scurry round tidying up frantically, standing breathlessly before the Queen's brightly polished metal mirror to smooth her hair and adjust the modest neck of her gown.

As she gazed at her reflection, she began to wonder for the first time whether it was all worth while. She worked hard to be sure, but nothing she did was right. She slept in a dormitory with the other maids of honour, and hated the lack of privacy and the continual presence of laughing, romping girls. But it would not have mattered if only one or two of the girls had been her friends. As it was, they either ignored or despised her. They thought her vain, and mocked her distaste for some of the tasks it was her duty to perform.

It was an honour, they told her, to dress and undress the Queen's ageing body; to spend hours mixing horrid concoctions of egg-white, powdered lime and lemon juice to smear over her Majesty's face, whitening an already pale complexion. Wrinkles were filled in, scrawny collarbones hidden beneath necklaces of gemstones, shape given to the Queen's amazing leanness by corsets that creaked like a coach whenever she moved hastily. When the Queen finally sailed forth from her withdrawing chamber, powdered, painted, prinked and overdressed to the point of absurdity, then and only then could the maids of honour relax.

Standing in the now empty room, drearily trying to make her sleeves hang evenly, the little Sydenham made a mental catalogue of the things and people she disliked most at court.

The nastiest girl, she decided, was Penelope Devereux, the beautiful golden-haired stepdaughter of the Queen's favourite, Robin Dudley. Penelope, she knew, was in love with Philip Sidney but betrothed to Richard, Lord Rich. Perhaps that was what made Penelope so sharp and spiteful to a girl who had no attachments at Court, but the little Sydenham did not think so. She thought Penelope enjoyed making witty remarks at the expense of someone young and unimportant.

The nastiest man was old Burghley, because he took no notice of her except to snap 'Fetch this,' or 'Find that,' at her whenever the Queen gestured for a task to be performed. She decided that Greenwich was the nastiest of the royal dwellings, though she had only been there, and to Richmond, where they were at present. The maids of honour suffered at Greenwich because of the lack of space so that temporary dwellings made of wood, with hard earth floors, had become permanent features, and in wet weather the rain crept in through ill-fitting windows and most of the passageways were unroofed anyway.

Out of so many unpleasant tasks, it was difficult to pick the nastiest, but the little Sydenham finally decided, with a shudder, that she hated applying colouring to her mistress's fading, puckered lips because her gums were swollen with some disease and, consequently, she supposed, her breath vile.

The sleeves were hanging as evenly as they ever would, and the little Sydenham remembered her duty with a sigh, and turned away from the mirror to make her way to the Presence Chamber. She would not be wanted, but she was sure to be missed if there was work to be done, and it was her duty to wait within call whilst the Queen conducted her interview with Francis Drake.

The door opened cautiously and a head poked into the room. Elizabeth jumped, guiltily, before she recognised Philip Sidney, and saw by the quick colour which flooded his face that he had not expected to find her there.

'The Queen has left, then?'

Elizabeth, smiling sweetly, said, 'Yes, my lord,' but she was thinking, it isn't the Queen whom Philip is hunting so assiduously. It's Penelope Devereux. However unpleasant Penelope might be to another female, nothing could exceed her charm where men were concerned. The big blue eyes would fill with soft expressive feeling, and her full lower lip

26

would tremble whenever a man came in sight. Elizabeth, used to thinking of herself as beautiful, found it hard to accept that beside Penelope she was like a candle beside the sun. Her small, slim body was immature compared to the rounded limbs and curvy figure of the eldest Devereux, and her face paled into insignificance when compared with the perfect features and rich colouring which Penelope possessed.

Perhaps I'll grow more beautiful as I mature, thought the little Sydenham, remembering that, after all, Penelope was three years older than herself. She would have been very surprised and flattered had she known that Sidney was looking at her with suddenly arrested attention.

What a charming child, he was thinking. So small, with such frail little bones. But lovely dark eyes full of feeling, and the way she had of folding her hands demurely and looking down her straight little nose seemed charming after the more obvious efforts made to attract his attention by the other maids of honour.

'Are you going to wait on the Queen? May I accompany you?' he asked, and was surprised at the rush of pink that coloured her cheeks, and the pleasure that suddenly made the dark eyes dance.

'Oh, yes, if you please, sir! Richmond is such a large place, I still find myself getting lost. I was afraid I'd missed the chance of seeing Francis Drake—he's a fellow Westcountryman of mine, you might say, for he's from Devon and I'm from Somerset. Of course, I've never been lucky enough to meet him though, even a quick glimpse of him through the crowd would be wonderful.'

Philip, smiling widely, held out an arm with his most elegant bow, and Elizabeth, her heart beating wildly, placed her hand, light as a moth, upon the velvet of his sleeve. Side by side they traversed the long corridors, and Philip was amused to notice that she was so small that he could see the parting in her dark hair—a clean straight line marching across her glossy crown.

'You're very silent, Mistress Sydenham,' he said at last, and was rewarded by the quick upward tilt of her head so that he saw her eyes, half wary, half excited.

'Yes, I'm not yet at ease in company,' admitted Elizabeth. 'I'm an only child, you know, and though I had a tutor there were very few children living near enough my home for me to become intimate with any one of them. So though I longed to come to Court, now that I'm here I often feel left out and unnoticed.'

For a moment, Sidney the poet was in the ascendant, and Sidney the ardent lover, who was determined to win Penelope Devereux, was forgotten. For the poet the clear, precise young voice speaking her mind without thought of coquetry was like a tumbling mountain brook. Penelope he loved for her extravagant beauty and the promise of ultimate surrender he could read in her eyes. But this child, he realised, was more mistress of herself than Penelope would ever be. For this one had scarcely thought of a man as a lover, whereas Penelope had never regarded men in any other light.

He found her refreshing, too, as she became more confident in his company and her face, which was too young to hide her feelings successfully, showed her disappointment and disillusion over the life of the Court. She was homesick, she confided, but she had learned not to admit as much to the other maids of honour, for fear of their mockery.

They arrived in the ante-chamber where the maids of honour clustered, playing cards, embroidering, and flirting with the young men around them. Philip's eye alighted on Penelope and immediately he forgot the little Sydenham. Murmuring, 'Excuse me,' he bowed with exquisite grace over her hand, touching it lightly with his lips and was gone, to join the crowd which surrounded Penelope to pay homage to her beauty.

Elizabeth stood still for a moment, feeling as if courage had been given her by his notice and kindness. Then she moved forward to join a knot of girls and men chatting idly by the impressive oak door leading into the Presence Chamber. She recognised Fulke Greville, Sidney's best friend, and smiled at him shyly. The Radcliffe sisters were there, and Elizabeth had often thought that she could be friendly with them if only she could cast her pride aside and talk freely to one or other of them. They kept themselves *to* themselves, that was the trouble. But now, perhaps, with the confidence newly born of her short talk with Philip Sidney, she would find the necessary courage.

As she joined them, the elder of the sisters, Jane, said kindly, 'This is our little Sydenham, Walter. We call her that because she is yet *another* Elizabeth, like my sister. The Queen calls *her* Radcliffe, as you know. Sydenham, this is Walter Ralegh, another of those infernal Westcountrymen. The place is thick with them today, all wild to see Francis Drake. But he's a relative of yours, isn't he, Walter?'

'Of a sort,' acknowledged Ralegh. 'But most Devonshire folk seem to be second or third cousins, or half-brothers or something.' He looked attentively at Elizabeth. 'You come from Combe Sydenham in Somerset, I take it? Sir George's only daughter?'

Elizabeth smiled and nodded, saying ruefully, 'But, alas, sir, Somerst folk don't seem to intermarry as much as you over the border, for I know no one in London—far less am I related to anybody at Court.'

Ralegh laughed. 'But my father married three times and my mother twice,' he said teasingly. 'Why, half of Devonshire cannot help but be related to me!'

'We Carews are kin of his, in some devious fashion,' said a fair young man in a mock-gloomy voice. 'But now that you come to mention it, lass, I'd say you are in a minority. Not many Devonshire squires send their daughters to Court.

They seem to marry them off young within the county.'

'Don't mind George,' Ralegh said airily. 'But I noticed you were squired by Philip Sidney a moment or two ago. Quite an honour, that, for he has his heart set on bedding Pen Devereux before the knot is tied between her and Lord Rich. They're laying bets on it, you know, but I wouldn't waste my money. She's got her mother to contend with, and the elegant Lettice still has all her wits about her. She knows she'll get no thanks from the rich Lord Rich if she barters damaged goods.'

The deep Devonshire burr did not take the sting out of the words, yet Elizabeth found herself laughing.

'As for poor Philip, his mother was a Dudley, so he's bound to have audacity, but his father, Sir Henry, sees it's well buried beneath good manners,' the impudent voice went on. 'Of course, Sidney will never break the marriage match; that's due to be consummated in a few weeks. But what is the good of laying bets on who will have the lady's virtue, when Sidney's such a perfect gentleman that he'd never tell?'

'Pooh, *we'd* know,' said Elizabeth Radcliffe at once. 'Penelope is dying to boast that Sidney is in truth her conquest—and as you well know, there is less honour than there should be in the ranks of her Majesty's maids of honour. Counting maidenheads in our dormitory wouldn't take two minutes, would it, Sydenham?'

Poor Elizabeth, who had often thought the same thing, felt the colour rush to her cheeks as the young men laughed at her confusion.

'Never mind them,' a tall man rather older than his companions said comfortingly, putting his arm round Elizabeth's narrow shoulders. 'Only a virgin could blush like that, eh, Walter?'

'My own experience of virgins is limited, Stukeley,' Ralegh said pensively. 'Now from what one hears of *your* experience ...'

But he did not finish the sentence. There was a stir in the doorway. Men and maids all stood back to allow the man who entered a free passage to the Audience Chamber where the Queen waited.

Elizabeth caught a glimpse of a short, sturdy man with hair bleached almost ginger by the sun, and skin as brown as a nut, and then the doors of the Presence Chamber opened, the man bowed deeply,

33

and as he walked towards the Queen the doors shut firmly behind him.

'Well, what did you think of my distant cousin, the Plague of Spain, the Pirate of Plymouth?' said Ralegh's voice close to Elizabeth's ear.

'Not what I expected,' admitted Elizabeth, her voice travelling further than she intended in the momentary hush. 'Full of character, I'll be bound, and very forceful—but much more ordinary than I had imagined.'

There was a general laugh and poor Elizabeth felt her cheeks flushing again. But George Carew said musingly, 'Yes, I know what you mean. He was gorgeously dressed and had the walk and air of a proud and independent man. But one expects heroic deeds to be accompanied by heroic aspect, which Francis Drake certainly doesn't possess. Our friend Ralegh here has the right looks, but, poor fellow, he suffers from seasickness, you know.'

Now the laughter was on Ralegh, but he shrugged it off with a satirical grin and the remark, 'Being seasick is damned unpleasant, but it's never stopped me from going a-voyaging, eh, Carew?'

'Nothing stops you from doing what you

want to do,' retorted George Carew. He turned to Elizabeth. 'Ralegh has been to Oxford, soldiered on the continent under one of his many relatives—Champernoun, was it not?—been befriended by Gascoigne, the soldier-poet, fought in Ireland and made pretty speeches to the Queen. But I assure you, Mistress Sydenham, that he's the most unruly, hot-tempered care-for-none who ever walked this good earth. They'll hang you yet, my proud fellow.'

'At least he'll have led a full life,' said Stukeley, grinning. 'And I'll be bound he makes such sharp remarks to the hangman that the rope is frayed, and the fellow loses all love for his trade.'

'I'll not be hanged,' Ralegh said indignantly. 'Maybe I'll be killed in a brawl, or a war—or maybe I'll have my head chopped off, like a gentleman. But I refuse to be hanged like a common pickpocket.'

'Yes, much more the thing to have your head chopped off,' said Stukeley sarcastically. 'But before you begin your execution speech, shall we settle down here, or shall we leave? Her Majesty will be unable to deal with such a fellow as Drake in less than an hour, I'll warrant.'

'I'm waiting,' said Ralegh decidedly. 'I

wouldn't miss a glimpse of the great man for all the gold in the Spanish treasure ships.'

'I have to wait,' Elizabeth pointed out. 'However, if you wish to play cards, gentlemen, I'll go to the other maidens.'

She turned with considerable reluctance towards the group of girls talking and laughing by the log fire at the other end of the hall.

'No, sit and talk to us; tell us what it's like to wait on the Virgin Queen,' Ralegh encouraged her. He had no desire to play cards and knew that argument was less likely in mixed company, for he knew from past bitter experience that his hot temper might well lead him into a difficult position. The trouble was, of course, that he was still largely moved by impulse: someone annoyed him, he had a glass of wine in his hand, then the wine would be thrown into the face of the opponent. From the top of his curly head to the tip of his heel, Walter Ralegh was a boiling ferment of feeling that must now and then overflow into verse, lovemaking, or violence. Yet his friends understood this and loved him, despite a tongue so sharp that it made him enemies without his being aware of it, and a temper so hot and uncontrolled that he led the gentlest into brawls.

But Elizabeth knew none of this. She merely saw a young man who was more handsome than she had believed possible, and who would help her to forget she was lonely for a brief hour. Thankfully, she rejoined the men and they settled themselves comfortably near the door, to wait for their hero.

★ ★ ★ ★

'Six hours he kept the Queen in conversation—imagine it—six hours!' Eleanor Wyatt pulled a wooden comb through long honey-gold hair and flicked her eyes expressively to the girl who sat near her.

'Imagine what they must have talked *about*, Eleanor! Why, Walter Ralegh was sitting with me, and it was all his friends could do to stop him bursting into the Presence Chamber! He kept us entertained, though, with the tales he thought Drake was telling the Queen. Being related, he had already heard many of Drake's adventures on his voyage of circumnavigation, and Ralegh told of such marvels it would have been hard to believe from another's lips.'

Elizabeth Sydenham's eyes shone softly. She had been caught by Ralegh's wit and physical attraction so that she lay in his web like a small, bright fly, helpless should her captor eye her with desire. But, so far, he had not done so. And thinking it over, she believed that he was too much in love with adventure itself to have much time for a little girl from Somerset who thought him a hero already.

'Did you notice Drake's scar, Sydenham? I heard him talk that it was an arrow scar, where one of the savages aimed at him and the arrow actually grazed his cheek.'

'Yes, it's true, Ralegh said so. It shows up more because his face is so brown. Oh, do hurry up with your hair, Eleanor. Drake is to attend Court again, you know.'

Eleanor got up reluctantly and stood watching whilst Elizabeth brushed her hair smooth and put a billiment of ruby velvet in place.

'Why, Sydenham, that's a very pretty dress. Why are you taking such care?'

Elizabeth looked down with some satisfaction at the red velvet sleeves and low-cut partlet, thickly embroidered with roses.

The skirts of her gown were spread wide, over a kirtle of deep rose pink, and the necklace around her slim throat was enamelled gold, wrought in the likeness of rosebuds. Though she was still immature, her stiffly boned bodice had pushed her budding breasts into prominence and she thought with delight, soon I shall be a woman!

To Eleanor, however, she said impishly, 'I'm hoping Drake will notice me.'

Eleanor's look of frank disbelief was tempered by her saying, 'You do look your best, Sydenham. The rich red and the deep pink might make some girls look insignificant so that one noticed only the colours. But it's just right for you. I suppose it's because you have black hair, for such colours would never do for me.'

Another girl, walking past them, said mockingly, 'So you dress brightly to attract Drake's eye, do you, little Sydenham? What makes you think he'll notice you, anyway, with *us* all around him? You have a high opinion of yourself, my girl.'

Before, such remarks had made Elizabeth cringe with shame and discomfort. It was true, she realised, that her lack of inches made her inconspicuous and that a woman was admired for her height and proportions. But now she could tell herself firmly that whatever else might happen, several men had noticed her—and shown they found her entertaining company. For the Westcountrymen stuck together, and had begun to include 'the Somerset lass' in their number. And however tall and stately other maids of honour might be, Elizabeth was delightfully certain of one thing. Drake *had* noticed her. She had seen his glance roam across the room as he left the Queen, and settle on her for one heart-stopping moment. Then he turned to a friend and no doubt she had been forgotten. But she felt confusedly that it was something to treasure—that this man who thought so little of women had spared her a glance of undoubted appreciation.

She smiled at her reflection and turned away from the mirror to join the other maids of honour, who were already beginning to go down to dinner in small groups.

Perhaps someone else will notice me, she thought, and the daring idea of deliberately attracting attention to herself brought a rose to her cheeks to match her kirtle. Hopefully, she tripped down the stairs.

3

THE KNIGHTING OF A CORSAIR

'The Queen is to knight Francis Drake, Sydenham! We shall be there—ah, how the Spaniards will grind their teeth with rage and fear! We are to journey to Deptford where Drake's ship, the *Golden Hind*, has been made ready to receive the Queen. Your first travel with the Court, my girl. You'll learn a lot about her Majesty's capricious ways, if nothing else.'

Elizabeth looked up at Dorothy Howard a trifle sourly. 'Need I know more of the Queen's capricious ways?' she demanded. 'Now I suppose we shall spend ages packing a vast number of garments which the Queen will probably never wear, and be allowed five minutes to scramble a few petticoats and kirtles into a bag for ourselves.'

Elizabeth was not much mistaken. The Queen, in an orgy of extravagance probably brought about by her share of

41

the treasure, had the most magnificent garments prepared. Ruffs so high and wide that she could scarcely turn her head from side to side; Spanish farthingales so big that the seamstresses prophesied glumly that their wearer would never squeeze aboard the *Golden Hind;* slippers encrusted with gems so that the petticoats had to be lifted whenever possible in order to show them off; all these things and more had to be carefully packed away by the patient maids of honour.

But all the time she toiled, the little Sydenham had a thought which brought a glow of contentment to her eyes. She had one very real admirer, Sir William Courtenay, another of the Devonshire men to whom Ralegh had introduced her. And she had to admit, she found him attractive. He was tall and rakish, with a reputation for womanising which made even the most forward girl eye him cautiously.

He was a ward of court and had spent most of his life outside Devonshire, Ralegh had told her. But his estates lay outside Exeter, and whilst at court he automatically joined his fellow Westcountrymen. He had first seen the little Sydenham in her ruby velvet with the rose-pink kirtle, and had wasted no time in making himself acquainted. He called her 'my Somerset rose', and though he said sweet things and paid charming compliments, there was that in his eye which warned Elizabeth he'd not be content for ever with a merely social relationship.

So though she looked forward to the visit to Deptford, it was with a certain amount of doubt. The little Sydenham knew from the talk in the maidens' dormitory that it was nothing new for a maid of honour to lie with a man: nor was it unheard of for a girl to retire to her father's country estates and give birth to a child. Sometimes the girl returned to Court unwed, to try again to get herself a husband. More often, however, the girl's father 'persuaded' the young man responsible to marry his daughter, which made everyone comfortable again. Except, thought Elizabeth, the young man!

But what of herself? Even a short while at Court had taught her that she was young for her age; she would not have the self-assurance to carry on an *affaire* with a man under the Queen's nose, as Dorothy Howard, her sister, and many of the other maids of honour did without a qualm.

On the slow progress to Deptford, passing through open countryside and streets lined with cheering citizens, Elizabeth managed to manoeuvre her horse near to Jane Radcliffe's so that they could talk in comparative privacy.

'Jane, why are there so few virgins in the dormitory?' she said curiously.

Jane laughed. 'Gracious, Sydenham, what a thing to ask! Are you thinking of joining the bedding brigade?'

'No, I'm too young,' said Elizabeth seriously. 'But why, Jane, do so many girls court disaster by sleeping with young men before marriage?'

This time Jane did not laugh, but said with a frankness that matched Elizabeth's own, 'Well, love, many of the young men at Court are nobles who either own large estates, or will do so some day. They want to be sure of wedding a girl who will give them fat and healthy babies to carry on their name.' She chuckled, and looked sideways at her friend. 'Also, Miss Innocence, men enjoy lying with a pretty maid, and it would be a strange girl who does not enjoy the embraces of the man of her choice. Does that answer your question?'

'Partly. But why don't you ...'

'Stop, stop, you inquisitive monkey,' cried Jane. 'My father holds an honourable position and can dower my sister and I well enough for most men. He has a match in mind for both of us, you impudent minx!'

'Is it a match of your choice?' asked Elizabeth curiously, and was sorry to see her friend's face cloud for a moment.

'Not exactly, no. An older man than I would have chosen. But one who is willing to wait whilst I enjoy the rest of this year at Court. And though perhaps he is not handsome, though he is a widower with several children, he is wealthy and kind. Now let's forget about marriage and enjoy this occasion—the Queen is certainly doing so!'

It was true. The Queen glittered almost as brightly with triumph as she did with jewels. By her side rode the French envoy, Marchaumont, who had come to arrange for the Duc d'Alencon to sue in person for the Queen's hand.

Jane sighed. 'The Queen really does seem to have everything, doesn't she?' she said rather wistfully. 'More magnificent clothes than anyone else in the kingdom, a hosts of adoring young men at her beck and call, some of the most beautiful jewellery in the world, servants and the excitement of being a dearly loved ruler. And now it seems as though she will have a young husband, too, lusty and frolicsome, who will restore the one thing she lacks—youth. Though she really doesn't look her age, does she?'

'No, you'd not take her for forty-seven, despite the rubbish we smear on her face,' admitted Elizabeth. 'She's terribly thin and active, and when her suitor sees her for himself, if he really does come, he'll probably be pleasantly surprised. But as for the Queen, she's liable to find him lustful rather than lusty, from what I've heard! The men say his sexual appetite is enormous, and once he's bedded the Queen he'll start working his way through the maids of honour! What excitement for us, eh, Jane?'

'Hush, someone may hear you,' murmured Jane nervously. 'But I dare say it's all talk, for no matter how the English hate the Spanish, they don't love the French, either. Anyhow, you know the Queen. Blow hot, blow cold; love, hate; marry tomorrow, die a virgin. No one knows her mind, not even the Earl of Leicester or old Burghley. Not even herself!'

But Elizabeth was not listening. She was leaning forward on her mare's neck, straining her eyes ahead. She thought she could see the glint of water, and the sun shining down from the bright April sky seemed to be reflected in the vivid new paint of a vessel.

'Jane, I do believe we've arrived!' she cried excitedly. 'Yes, oh, yes! I can see Francis Drake standing on the deck of his little ship tricked out in the finest gear with a ruff almost as big as the Queen's! I mean Drake's wearing a ruff, not the ship, silly. Can you see?'

'I can indeed, Sydenham. Quick, dismount and hand the reins to one of the stable lads. We don't want to be left on shore whilst the others go on board with the Queen.'

The two girls slipped from their saddles and hurried towards the glistening vessel, whilst ahead of them they could see the glittering, diademed head of the Queen, the neat dark hair of Marchaumont, and the light, reddish hair of the French Ambassador, Mauvissiere. Around the three principal figures swarmed the tall, swaggering young men of the Court with whom the Queen loved to talk and laugh.

There was a slight delay as the Queen stepped aboard which nearly drove Elizabeth wild, for she was so small that not a thing could she see, though she could hear the Queen's high, excited laugh.

'Missing the excitement? Up with you, little one,' exclaimed a familiar voice, and Elizabeth felt strong hands round her waist and before she could do more than squeak with surprise, she was hoisted shoulder high by Sir William Courtenay so that she could see the scene for herself.

'The Queen dropped her violet velvet garter,' Courtenay explained, 'And that little frog, Marchaumont, picked it up and said he would carry it back to the Duc d'Alencon for a keepsake. What's happening now, my Somerset rose? I can't see through you!'

'She's shaking her head and laughing, holding out her hand for the garter,' reported Elizabeth, grabbing the short curly hair of her companion's crown to make her perch more secure and ignoring his anguished 'Ouch!'

'Don't tear my hair out by the roots, and don't wriggle, or I'll drop you,' warned

Courtenay, squeezing his burden more tightly. 'What's she doing now?'

'Ooh, if one of us did that we'd get a clip over the ear from the Queen,' Elizabeth reported with a muffled giggle. 'Marchaumont has handed over the garter and the Queen has dragged up her skirt—well, very high, I can tell you, and she's putting her garter on again with everyone watching. Now Marchaumont can carry back the news that she's got very pretty, shapely legs to his master, as well as the rest.'

'Anything else, or are they moving on board?'

'You can put me down, they're going on to the ship,' said Elizabeth. She turned in Courtenay's arms and slid on to the ground, aware that the closeness of his body excited her, as the nearness of her own young limbs excited him. For a moment he held her round the waist, then he released her and helped her to make her way near to the ship.

'No one else will be allowed aboard her now, you know,' he said kindly, seeing the little Sydenham's face fall. 'But after the banquet I'll show you over the ship, if you'd like to see it.'

'If you go with him, you're a fool, Sydenham,' admonished Ralegh, standing near by. 'His reputation is worse than mine—you'd find yourself in the captain's bed before you'd had time to turn round, and not with the captain, either.'

He and Courtenay smiled at one another. 'Takes a rogue to know one,' commented Courtenay cheerfully. 'Come on, then, let's make our way to the banqueting tables.'

The banquet was the most magnificent Elizabeth had ever imagined. Everyone was laughing and excited, hearts high because the cautious, clever lady who ruled by charm and will-power was letting her feelings get the better of her inborn caution. She was going to knight Drake, whom the Spaniards called 'El Draque' at best, and corsair, pirate, rogue and heretic at worst. And by doing so she would show Philip, as nothing else could, what she thought of him and his people, and who was master of this small but brave country of hers.

Ralegh, serving the Queen, who sat at the high table with Drake and a chosen few, said hurriedly as he passed the little Sydenham, 'Mark my words, we'll be at war with Spain before the year is out! Old

Mendoza gnashed his teeth with rage and screamed at Elizabeth when she said she was not going to punish Drake, because Spaniards had landed in Ireland which is a part of her realm. Then he was fool enough to lose his temper and threaten her with war. Fire blazed one moment, ice glinted the next! Chris Hatton was there and he swears the room went cold! He says there was a short silence and then the Queen said, quite quietly, 'If you talk to me like that again, I'll put you in a place where you cannot talk at all.' Don Bernardino went green and began to stammer something, but the Queen dismissed him and he had to leave.'

'Goodness, I'd hate to be snubbed by her Majesty,' Elizabeth said to Jane, as Ralegh left them. 'It's dreadful when she flies into a temper, and boxes ears and hurls anything that comes handy at our heads. But somehow it's more natural than the iciness that Ralegh described.'

'Look lively, they're leaving the table,' warned Jane. 'Now if we stand aside politely as Drake leads her Majesty aboard the ship and then move like lightning, we'll get a place near the front of the crowd and see with our own eyes the Queen knighting

Drake with the gilded sword.'

By dint of pushing and shoving, they wormed their way to the front, to stand near the young gentlemen of Devon, who had made sure of a good place, the girls suspected, by leaving the table before the Queen and her escort.

But to everyone's surprise, the Queen handed the heavy state sword to the Frenchman, saying with an impish smile, 'The Spaniards have demanded the head of this gallant gentleman, Monsieur. But England has need of him still. Therefore, perhaps you, as a Frenchman, had better knight my Master Mariner, or he might fear I was about to execute him.'

'This is really going too far,' said Ralegh with a wicked grin. 'God, Carew, when you think how the Spaniards hate the French and the English, she goes too far.' But the little Sydenham, quietly watching Ralegh's lean, excitable face, thought he did not look annoyed about it—quite the opposite, in fact.

'Perhaps the Queen is making up for the indignity suffered by his countryman, the French Ambassador, last year,' suggested Jane with a smile.

Ralegh gave a muffled crow of laughter

and George Carew grinned reluctantly. Seeing the question in Elizabeth's eyes he said, 'Did you not hear about the dreadful affair in Smithfield? It was after the Queen had decreed that gentlemen were wearing their ruffs too large and magnificent. She appointed a number of officers who hung about the streets and were supposed to stop any passers-by whose ruff exceeded certain limits, by clipping them with shears, as though they were sheep whose wool hung too heavy.'

'They also had orders to clip rapiers that were overlong,' Ralegh chipped in, his mouth solemn but his eyes dancing. ' "Heaven save me from having my rapier clipped," was the cry at Court!'

Elizabeth gurgled with amusement at the absurd story and Carew frowned at her, though his lips twitched.

'Don't laugh, wench. It's no more than the truth, and might have led to an international incident. Not only ruffs (nor only rapiers!) might have been severed. For, you see, the stately and dignified Mauvissiere was taking his morning constitutional in Smithfield when he was stopped by certain of these ruff-shearers and bidden to hold still whilst they cut him down to size.'

Elizabeth's laughter had to be muffled in her handkerchief and even Jane, who knew the story well, was smiling broadly.

'But the noble Ambassador was not to be so shorn,' continued Carew blandly. 'He drew his sword and defied the officers of the Crown. Heaven knows what might have happened had not an English gentleman of the Court been riding by. Walsingham, wasn't it? Well, anyway, he went to poor Mauvissiere's aid, and the Queen had to apologise most humbly for her men's lack of discrimination in picking on the jewel of the French Court for clipping. But I'll be bound she did it with her tongue in her cheek, for the Queen has a rare sense of humour,' he finished, grinning.

'How brave of the man—was it really Walsingham?—to take the Frenchman's part,' said Elizabeth. 'Why, he might have had his ruff shorn as well!'

'Better to lose an inch or two from your ruff than embroil your country in a horrid war. Imagine it—soldiers armed with shears, each man intent on protecting his own ruff,' said Ralegh, watching as Elizabeth wailed with helpless mirth at the imaginary spectacle.

'The man was Henry Seymour, and well you both know it,' said Jane, smiling. 'Now stop being absurd, you two, and watch, for the sword is about to descend and the Queen's Master Mariner will become Sir Francis.'

Attentive and silent now, they watched as the Frenchman tapped Drake lightly on each shoulder. Then the Queen cried, 'Rise up, Sir Francis Drake,' and he got quickly to his feet and bent low over the slim, outstretched hand.

When the Queen left the ship, a small body of young men lingered, with Elizabeth and Jane still in their midst. Drake gazed at them from oddly piercing blue eyes, his glance amused. It was, typically, Ralegh who spoke first.

'We honour you and we envy you, Sir Francis,' he said softly. 'Not only for your exploits and daring, but for the humanity you have shown to enemies who would have shown none to you.'

Sir Francis looked pleased and confused. Ralegh had gone unerringly to the most important point, by Drake's standards. People. He held no life lightly, neither that of his humblest sailor nor the sloppy Spanish slut whom the townspeople had once pushed outside their gates before barring them against the English. Life was a sacred trust and one did not take such a trust lightly.

'Many would throw Doughty's death at my head rather than praise my humanity,' Drake said at last. He had to look up to meet Ralegh's eyes, yet suddenly it seemed to Elizabeth that the two men were equal, even to stature.

'Doughty was convicted at a fair trial on a charge of treason. You could not have been expected to keep him aboard, in danger of stirring up a mutiny,' protested Sidney, and Elizabeth realised for the first time that he, too, had stayed behind with the other men.

But it was still to Ralegh that Drake looked, and Ralegh said in his deep voice, 'I must have the gentleman to haul and drew with the mariner, and the mariner with the gentleman.'

Drake nodded slowly. 'Aye. My very words. Every man aboard my ship will vouch for them. You are ...?'

'Walter Ralegh, sir.'

'Come to my cabin, Ralegh. We must talk.'

The two men disappeared, and the little

group on deck stirred as though they had been dreaming and were beginning to wake up.

'How strange it was to hear Ralegh say those words. They meant a lot to Drake, didn't they?' ventured Elizabeth at last.

Carew nodded soberly. 'Yes. For it's my belief that in those words rather than in all the grand accusations and counter-accusations lie the truth behind Doughty's execution. Drake is Sir Francis now, but then he was just a mariner—or perhaps I should say master mariner, as the Queen did. Doughty was a gentleman adventurer, and though not fitted to lead, thought that *because* he was a gentleman and Drake was not, he ought to be given a bigger share of the command. So he suggested to other such "gentlemen" that they band together against the commoner in their midst. Praise be to God, the others realised that Doughty was inferior to their commander—and a danger also. But Drake will feel that death heavy upon his mind for many months to come.'

By mutual consent, the little party lingered on the deck of the *Golden Hind* until Sir Francis brought Ralegh back into the fast fading light of that memorable day.

He greeted them jovially, saying to Philip Sidney, 'Young Ralegh tells me you're a poet. Here's a strange place to find such a one, on the deck of my little ship.'

'A poet can only write of what he has experienced, or knows,' said Sidney shyly. 'I'd give much to journey as you have done—not for treasure alone, nor yet even for England's glory, but for the sake of the sights you've seen.'

'Well, maybe you'll sail with me one day, now that her Majesty has made it plain to all good Englishmen that it is no crime to rob from the robber-Spaniards,' Drake said cheerfully.

'Will you sail again soon, Sir Francis?' Elizabeth asked timidly, and was pleased when the piercing blue gaze found her, and softened. She did not know that he took her for a mere child, and was thinking: Such a one I might have called daughter, had Mary and I been blessed with children.

But he answered her gently, aware of her flushed cheeks, and the hands which twisted together at her own boldness.

'I cannot stop from sailing, Mistress. But it's time I settled down for a while. I shall buy some property in the country

and spend more time with my poor Mary
(goodness, she's Lady Mary now; how
that will please her!), for she has waited
patiently for me in the past.'

His smile embraced them all, but his
eyes lingered longest on Ralegh. They were
so different, yet they had many things in
common. He liked the lad.

Then he raised his hand in farewell and
turned to go into his cabin.

'Hell's teeth, if the Queen sees we've
lingered there'll be trouble,' said Ralegh,
suddenly coming down to earth with a
jolt. 'Two maidens in our midst—ah well,
there's safety in numbers, they say. But
we'd better get back to the rest of the
royal party before we're missed.'

As they mounted their horses Elizabeth
said softly to Ralegh, 'Where is Sir William
Courtenay, Ralegh? He was with us in the
crowd earlier in the day, but he didn't
linger with us, to talk to Drake.'

Ralegh was quick to notice the slight
pique in her voice and his teeth glinted
in a sardonic smile which brought a slight
colour to her cheeks.

'Maybe he's found a maid willing to
exchange more than glances,' he said
wickedly. 'But no doubt he'll not have

strayed far from the Queen, so we'll catch up with him presently.'

'I don't care,' said Elizabeth, trying to look indifferent. 'I just wondered. We'd better hurry, for even if *I'm* not missed, her Majesty would soon notice the absence of her wild Westcountrymen.'

★ ★ ★ ★

In the days that followed, William Courtenay kept up his siege on the little Sydenham's citadel. He talked and laughed with her whenever the opportunity occurred, pulled her into curtained alcoves to kiss her and squeeze her slender waist, and generally made it fairly obvious that she had caught his fancy.

Elizabeth, for her part, was none too sure of her own feelings. She knew that Courtenay excited her and she enjoyed both his company and his embraces. But she felt little of the affection and admiration for him that other men, such as Philip Sidney and Walter Ralegh, had roused in her susceptible breast.

Then, suddenly, Courtenay found his opportunity—and Elizabeth discovered exactly how she felt. It happened on a fine day in early summer. A party of young people had wandered off into the country together, to gather flowers and sweet-smelling herbs for the palace, but really to enjoy the sweet air and each other's company. Philip Sidney did not have Penelope Devereux to walk with, for Penelope's mother had carried her daughter off to be married to Lord Rich. But Philip and Greville walked together in perfect amity, with Courtenay and Elizabeth following them.

When Courtenay said, 'Look, little Sydenham, wild roses!' Elizabeth followed him into the belt of trees knowing, she thought, perfectly well what his intentions were. However, she had underrated him. In a manner she afterwards decided was far too practised, he swung her off her feet and laid her on the soft dry grass under the trees. Then, with amazing dexterity, he proceeded to begin pulling off her bodice, whilst almost smothering her with kisses and pressing his hard, athletic body against her.

Elizabeth was small and slight, but she found a strength she had not known she possessed. A hand clawed wildly at his face, then found his hair and tugged hard. As his mouth was jerked back for an instant she gave a small, fierce shriek and then gave her attention to the task of freeing herself from the burden of his body, which was suddenly terrifying and distasteful.

Sidney and Greville, deep in talk, heard the shriek and returned up the path at a trot.

'Should we interfere?' Fulke Greville said rather doubtfully. 'Women are such strange creatures, she may be enjoying seduction for all we know.'

Sidney gave him a glance of amused contempt. 'She's a baby, the little Sydenham. Come on.' He and Fulke plunged into the thicket from which the yell had sounded.

It says much for Courtenay's ardour that it took the full strength of both young men to pull him from Elizabeth's furiously writhing body—and that once detached, so to speak, he tried very hard to pick a fight with Philip Sidney for what he termed 'spoiling the pleasure of a man with a maid'.

Elizabeth, humiliatingly conscious of crumpled clothes, a torn bodice, a hanging sleeve that was not *meant* to hang, and twigs in her hair, could only lean on the comforting strength of Fulke Greville's arm and long to be safe in the maidens' dormitory.

'Take her away, Fulke,' ordered Sidney quickly. 'I should get her tidied up a bit first, or someone might leap to the right conclusions and that would mean trouble for everyone from the Queen.' He turned to Courtenay. 'God, man, don't you find enough women at Court who will lie with you, without trying to rape a maid of honour still in her green youth? For your own good, don't linger here at Court. Go back to your Devon estates—I know such a move is in the wind, and must suppose that's the reason you treated the little Sydenham so. Will you apologise?'

Courtenay was picking bits of grass and earth off his hose, but he smiled at Elizabeth and said earnestly, 'I *do* apologise, my Somerset rose. You see, Sidney knows a man's weaknesses. I'm to return to Devon to run my estates and marry the wife who has been chosen for me. I had done my utmost to win your father over to helping me to break the betrothal which has been made for me, but he thinks you too young for marriage. Will you forgive me?'

'It will be easier to do so if you leave the Court at once,' said Elizabeth reluctantly. 'My father is right, I *am* too young for marriage—too young to lie with you in a wood, either.'

Courtenay grimaced. 'I'll go at once,' he promised. 'My servants can send my gear after me. Now you, my little rose, will be plucked by another. How much sweeter could our love have been.'

But Elizabeth, standing like a subdued child whilst Fulke Greville tidied her up, was privately of the opinion that nothing could be nastier than her recent experience. If that was a prelude to marriage, what horrors lay in wait for her in the marriage bed? She could only shudderingly promise herself that in future she would be the most cold-eyed and tight-lipped maid of honour that the Elizabeth Court had ever known.

In marriage, she knew, the woman must submit to her husband. But at least she would be walking knowingly into the experience; it would not have all the horrors of surprise that had accompanied William Courtenay's amorous attack.

Greville, having straightened her gown and tidied her hair with considerable embarrassment (for he was no ladies' man), escorted her back to the palace and saw her safely to the foot of the stairs leading to her quarters. As he bade her farewell, he was surprised to see that her face wore a slightly mischievous smirk. He would have been even more surprised had he been able to read the thoughts that had conjured up such an expression.

When I marry, and lie naked in bed with a man, at least I shan't have his beastly buttons and fastenings bruising my breasts, or his shod feet trampling on my ankles, ran Elizabeth's thoughts. Nor will I have half my mind on his dreadful activities and the other half on the demi-train of my gown, which was getting sadly crushed!

4

MARRIAGE TO ENGLAND'S HERO

'So your swain who is so fearless when he strides the deck of his ship is still silent?' said Eleanor Wyatt teasingly. She was betrothed to be married herself, and she and Elizabeth had grown close in the course of the four years they had been at Court.

Drake, whose wife Mary had died the year after the little Sydenham had first met him, had soon made it obvious that he enjoyed her company. Gradually, it was realised round the Court that the little Sydenham was the only girl whom Sir Francis ever sought out; and when she was talking and laughing with someone else, a pair of keen blue eyes in a tanned face were apt to follow her movements closely.

Elizabeth acknowledged that she was flattered; that she liked her heroic admirer. Further than that she was not prepared to go—and for a very good reason. She did not believe that Drake was considering re-marriage with anyone. He had told her shortly after his wife's death that he had been a poor sort of husband to Mary Newman.

'I married a shy, pretty, affectionate woman,' he told Elizabeth remorsefully. 'But did I help her to overcome her shyness? Not I! Too busy with my ships and my desire for adventure. Then I tried to deck her out in foreign silks and satins, and folk were so struck by my poor bird's fine feathers that they scarcely noticed her pretty looks. And what outlet did she have for her affection? *I* gave her no children; little of my own company, even. Seeking after wealth and excitement and fame, absorbed by masculine pursuits. Then when I decide to stay in England for a while, it was all London, the Court, important office and great houses for me. I scarcely noticed Mary growing paler, until I found her near death, vomiting blood in the kitchens of my fine new house, with only a maidservant for company, so that she should not worry me! Much good I had done her with my wealth and my gifts. She should have married a sturdy yeoman farmer who could have given her children to love, and his affection and attention, rather than a man who left her lonely. I was a poor husband, Liza.'

So Elizabeth accepted his attentions gracefully and waited impatiently to see what would be her lot in life. She knew her father believed Drake was going to offer for her; he had received other offers, and turned them down.

She did not mind the teasing of Eleanor, who was her friend, but she minded very much the sidelong glances of others; the marrying of girls younger and less pretty than she. The Howard girls had married, Mary Wriothsley had married ... two years earlier, Sir Philip Sidney had apparently forgotten his grief over Penelope Devereux's marriage to Lord Rich, and taken to wife a little fourteen-year-old—Frances Walsingham, the younger daughter of Sir Francis Walsingham, the Queen's trusted secretary. Of course, everyone who *was* anyone knew that Sidney and Penelope Rich were lovers, and that even after his marriage their *affaire* continued. But nevertheless, it was also common knowledge that the little Sydenham continued pure as a lily though she was getting on for eighteen, and though Sir Francis Drake danced attendance on her he was apparently content to do so indefinitely.

But now Elizabeth jerked her thoughts back to the present, to answer Eleanor.

'He has not spoken yet,' she admitted. 'But I'm sure he'll either ask for me within the next week, or never. My father would like to see me married to Drake, but even he grows tired of waiting for Sir Francis to make up his mind whether to remarry or remain a widower. Another gentleman has asked me to marry him and I've told him to tell Father that I'm tired of the Court and wish for a home of my own. If Sir Francis doesn't make up his mind quickly, then he will be too late, for I'll marry the other.'

'You're a strange girl, Sydenham,' Eleanor said thoughtfully. 'You've never said whether you love Sir Francis, and you don't say you love this other suitor. Who is he, by the way?'

'Fulke Greville,' said Elizabeth, pride and mirth blending in her voice. 'He's always been fond of me and I like him very much, but to tell the truth I think he's lonely now that Sir Philip is so busy with a wife and mistress. As for *love*—oh, I don't know, Eleanor. What is love, after all? When I first came to Court I thought myself in love—first with Sir Walter Ralegh (though he hadn't been knighted then) and later with Sir William Courtenay. Ralegh was just like Drake in a way—he has to be where the excitement is. I've scarcely seen him during the past three years, he's always off on some wild escapade. Courtenay is married and has children. Other men have stirred my blood, but my father has said the marriage would not be suitable. Now I feel I must force his hand. I've no intention of growing old as a maid of honour, I can assure you.'

'You're not cold, Sydenham. Yet you will marry where your father bids. Ah well, most of us are the same, I suppose. But suppose Drake *were* to decide to take the plunge into a second marriage. How would you feel then?'

'I should feel very proud—for he'll only marry when he's absolutely certain that he is doing the right thing,' said Elizabeth positively. 'He will marry for love, that I swear. If he loves me enough to marry me, then I shall soon love him, Eleanor. But I don't intend to live with a broken heart because I've fallen in love with the wrong man. No, I'm not cold. That's part of my trouble. I could easily become as wanton as—as a Howard, given the opportunity. So it's marriage or nothing for me, my girl.'

And in a remarkably short space of time, marriage it was. Sir Francis Drake might not have a pedigree as long as the noble family of Sydenham of Combe Sydenham, but he was rich, famous, and, furthermore, Elizabeth Sydenham had made it plain that should Sir Francis wish to marry her and should her father take it into his head to be difficult, she would either run off with Sir Francis, or marry the first stableboy to take her fancy.

Now that the marriage date was settled, Elizabeth thought with a shiver of appreciation that, before, she had known only Sir Francis Drake the courtier, dressed to impress the Queen and perhaps herself. Now she would know the man—what he was like at breakfast; whether he had a quick temper; whether he had a sense of humour. She would see for herself how highly (or otherwise, of course!) they thought of him in his native town of Plymouth.

* * * *

As soon as the marriage settlements were arranged, to the mutual pleasure of Sir Francis Drake and Sir George Sydenham, Elizabeth moved back to Combe Sydenham to prepare for her wedding in the small neighbouring church of Monksilver.

Lady Elizabeth gave her daughter a few words of motherly advice on a satisfactory bedding which were wasted on Elizabeth, who had not lived at Court for nearly four years without getting to know the facts of life. Then she was walking sedately down the aisle of the church on Sir Francis' arm, with murmurs of 'Good luck, milady,' and 'All happiness and many children to you both,' coming from the mouths of those who had known her since childhood.

They would spend the first night of their married life at Sydenham Castle, then they would ride slowly down to Plymouth, staying in the homes of friends and in Sir Francis' own manors on the way.

* * * *

Their arrival in Plymouth made Elizabeth

feel like royalty. The town was walled, and as they rode under the arch of the gateway leading from Exeter a crowd of eager citizens surged towards them, to cheer the bride and their hero.

Elizabeth, smiling happily, was glad that the early spring sun was shining on her beautiful lawn head-dress, glad that her gown though severely cut for riding became her well, glad too that her husband showed such obvious pride in his new wife.

'Why, are we to live near the sea?' she cried to Drake, and he answered, smiling, 'There is scarce a house in Plymouth which is not near the sea, my darling, for the town is surrounded on three sides by water. See?'

He indicated with a broad sweep of his arm the glittering expanse of sea which could be seen between the houses, then added, 'We'll go to my house in High Street and you can change your dress and have some refreshment. Then I'll show you Plymouth.'

His proud tone made Elizabeth smile, but when she saw her new home her delight almost equalled that of her husband.

A beautiful town house, newly built, with its timbers gleaming pale gold against the whitened cob walls, the tiles shining bright as marigolds against the sky. Windows sparkled, each small leaded pane polished to within an inch of its life, and through the glass the servants' faces showed, oddly distorted and pale green, as they peered out to catch their first glimpse of the new mistress.

The horses were led through an arch into a neat cobbled yard surrounded by stables.

'There is a garden, small, but full of sweetly scented flowers,' Sir Francis told his wife as he helped her to dismount. 'You'll find most of your favourite blossoms there in the summer, though now it looks rather cold and bare.'

He led her indoors and into the front parlour, where a huge fire danced on the hearth and the walls were hung with exotic tapestries. The curtains at the windows, decided Elizabeth with her first thrill of housewifely pride, were *quite* the wrong colour. They were a dark shade of blue. They should be brighter, lighter, more in tune with the newness of the house. More *modern*, she thought triumphantly. Then her husband was leading her through the door and down three steps to the kitchen, which was another large room, with the latest baking ovens, windows opened wide to let out the steam, and the most delicious smells of cooking hovering in the warmed air.

Their tour continued with the inevitable visit to their bedchamber, where Isabelle already awaited her, glancing with curiosity at the magnificence of the marriage bed, with its soft pillows and lavender-scented sheets, and the long velvet bed-hangings which they would draw close when they climbed into bed later that night.

Rather to Elizabeth's amusement, she noticed that when Francis' eyes rested on their bed, a blush darkened his complexion for a moment. Then, with a bow and a smile, he turned and left the room so that Isabelle could help her mistress change out of her riding dress.

'Do you like the house, milady?' asked Isabelle, easing the bodice carefully from Elizabeth's breasts. Elizabeth herself un-hooked her gown and kirtle and stood in her shift and petticoat, looking out on to the clean little street which ran below the windows, for even the kennel where housewives usually dumped their rubbish had been swept in her honour.

'It's very charming; perfect for living in Plymouth. But Sir Francis says we shall spend most of our time at Buckland Abbey, a great mansion he owns some miles outside the town,' said Elizabeth airily, smiling at Isabelle's exclamation of pleasure.

'Shall you wear the seagreen, milady, with the tawny kirtle and matching sleeves?'

'Yes, anything,' said Elizabeth impatiently. 'Oh, do hurry, Belle, for Francis wants to show me the town of Plymouth and already the streets are filling up with every sort of person. Look, the streets of London are crowded by many, magnificently dressed, but somehow these men seem bigger, and more important.'

'It's the way they walk, as if they own the town,' said Belle, peering over her mistress's shoulder through the mullioned window. 'Lor', milady, some of 'em are brown as Spaniards!'

'Considering Sir Francis is tanned to a similar shade, I don't think that was a very tactful remark,' said Elizabeth, grinning. 'Come on, Belle, I'm clean, I'm dressed, except for the minor refinements such as gown and jewellery and a cloak. I don't want to keep Sir Francis waiting.'

So within the shortest time she could manage, the new Lady Elizabeth Drake was stepping briskly beside her husband, down the streets towards the harbour of Sutton Pool, where he had promised to show her all the shipping, and tell her about the craft, before strolling on to Cattewater to see St Nicholas' Island, recently fortified, and finally up the Hoe and back into the town.

They picked their way down the side of High Street, Elizabeth openly curious about their neighbours so that she could not resist a peep into the big windows to see what colour *their* curtains were, and whether they too had tapestries hanging on the walls, or had chosen to have their panelling painted.

Passers-by smiled kindly at her, thinking her a pretty piece, and lucky too, for had she not got the best man in Plymouth for her husband? Drake slowed his pace to hers, and pointed out the wells where he watered his ships—and where conduits ran down to the houses of the rich, bringing water to their very doors. They went down Southside Street, where the houses were fine buildings, and Sir Francis pointed out the home of the Hawkins family so that his Liza should know where his famous friend and cousin lived.

In New Street, building was still going on, but several of the houses were already occupied. Though less fine than her own home, Elizabeth thought they were lucky to be so near the sea, for already she could hear the water lapping against the quay.

'They're pleasant, comfortable dwellings,' Sir Francis admitted. 'And built by a friend of mine, John Sparke. He knows when and how to make a pretty penny, does John. For with the Queen's consent to my—er—treasure-seeking, mariners from all over the county—nay, all over England —want to have a home in Plymouth where they are near the centre of all things maritime.'

As he spoke they stepped out on to the quayside and the sparkling waters of Sutton Pool were at their feet, ruffled by the wind with its nip of winter to remind them that the month was only February, yet set a-dancing by the pale sunshine.

'There, on those beaches,' said Sir Francis, pointing, 'are where the ship-builders ply their trade. They build some of the best ships in the world here, my love.

Sutton Pool must be about the safest and yet easiest place to build boats, for there is no tortuous river to negotiate, to slow you down so that the enemy knows of your plan to sail almost as soon as you do yourselves. I'll take you to have a closer look at the building another day, though. Now let us walk round to the Hoe and you shall see the magnificent fortifications young William Hawkins caused to be built on St Nicholas' Island. Well, I call him young, for he's younger than John, his brother. But to a pretty child like you he'll seem old, for he's nine or ten years older than me.'

He glanced at his wife's profile and looked quickly away again, and Elizabeth thought: He's awfully conscious that he's older than me. If he wanted a wife nearer his own age, why did he marry me? I certainly didn't make him.

She was beginning to feel very uneasy.

However, the brisk walk with the wind off the sea freshening as they came out of the shelter of the houses on to the Hoe made her forget her worries. She laughed aloud as the wind snatched her hair from her confining hood, and she saw it beginning to whip the water into white horses even within the comparative shelter of Plymouth Sound.

'Cattewater is ruffled like an angry cat, perhaps that's why it is so named,' she said, laughing, but Drake answered, 'The sky is clouding, little one. Come on, we'd better hurry back to our home before we get drenched to the skin.' His eyes dwelt on her fondly. 'I'm used enough to being soaked with brine and dried up with the sun, but you're a more delicate creature.'

He hurried her back home and once again led her into the wide-windowed parlour warmed by the huge fire. Friends were coming to visit them for their first dinner in Plymouth, so Elizabeth went upstairs to straighten her gown and comb her tangled curls. When she returned to the parlour, several couples had already arrived.

In the hum of introductions, talk and frankly curious stares, Elizabeth heard for the first time of a proposed voyage which was being planned for the summer months. When they sat down at table, the talk turned completely to the plans for this venture.

Elizabeth gathered that her husband was to lead an expedition ostensibly to seek for legitimate treasure, new lands and so on, but really to discourage Spain in her attempts against the Low Countries. Once Spain had conquered there, how easy it would be for King Philip to despatch his fleets against England! The Queen had no intention of sitting idly by whilst this happened—on the other hand, she had no intention of committing an act of war. So, once again, an act of aggression would be masked by more peaceful purposes. And there was always the hope of treasure!

'How will the fleet discourage the Spaniards from conquering the Low Countries?' Elizabeth asked her neighbour and brother-in-law, Thomas Drake. He glanced at her, a look of mingled annoyance and amusement. 'What a wonderful wife you make for a seaman, sister,' he said spitefully. 'Why, we shall destroy as much shipping as we can find so that Spain cannot send her troops across the ocean.'

'Of course,' said Elizabeth quickly. 'But if the expedition is to take place in the summer, why is everyone assembling in Plymouth in February?'

His sneer was open now. 'The work of preparation for a voyage is one of the hardest tasks of all. Victualling the ships—indeed, some are still being built—getting the men to sail them, choosing your captains, all these jobs take many months. And always there is the chance the Queen may change her mind and decide that, after all, the fleet shall not sail.'

Elizabeth looked confused. 'Yes, of course, Tom, how foolish I am!' she said. She was thinking to herself: I knew he didn't like me, I should not have asked him. But, oh dear, it's so painfully obvious *why* he doesn't like me! He's frightened out of his wits in case I give his brother an heir, which would ruin his chances of inheriting Drake's estate. Little does *he* know, evidently.

And presently, when the meal was over and the men sitting round the fire, talking the interminable talk of ships and the sea, Elizabeth curtsied to the company, kissed her husband respectfully, and announced that she was going to bed.

As she walked slowly up the steep stairs, she thought to herself: Five days married, and still a virgin! If this goes on much longer I'll never be a wife!

★ ★ ★ ★

Two hours later, Sir Francis was seeing his friends off at the front door, waving to their shadowed shapes as they moved away down the narrow street. They went towards the waterfront mainly, and momentarily the thought of all the work he had to do to prepare his fleet for sea satisfied his mind. Then he thought of his young wife, upstairs in the double bed, and his heart gave a startled leap.

What is the matter with me? he thought. He'd bedded Mary Newton without a second thought on their wedding night. But his Liza? She seemed so very young and innocent, with her face like a white flower amidst the dark masses of her hair. She had made no complaint when he had prayed on his knees all the night following their wedding, she had even offered to join him, but he had picked her up and laid her on the bed, already half-sleeping. She probably thought him gentle then, and generous too, to give up his pleasuring because she was tired and afraid. But what did she think of him now? He stumbled up the stairs, and cursed quietly beneath his breath.

She would be asleep by now. He could slip quietly into bed without disturbing her and perhaps by tomorrow night he would grow less afraid of hurting her; less nervous in case she found him distasteful, a rough sailor with little knowledge of the arts of lovemaking.

He opened the heavy oak door quietly and slipped into the room. The curtains were drawn round the bed, but he undressed without lighting the candle nonetheless, his movements quick and neat in the dim starlight. Stripped to his shirt, he trod cat-quiet over to the bed and listened. Her breath was like herself—light and steady. He pulled back the curtains and carefully eased his way between the sheets. In the warm darkness he snuggled down cautiously, preparing himself for sleep.

Then the young woman beside him moved, turning over so that she faced him, hunching up her knees and suddenly shooting them out straight so that before he could pull himself away he felt the warm firmness of her breasts pressing against him. Startled, he realised that she had discarded the shift that she had worn previously, leaving it on during the night for warmth. She was mother-naked and he wore only his plain undershirt.

Cautiously, he slipped his hand over and cupped her smooth, bare shoulder in his palm. She sighed and stirred, but did not wake. Suddenly, he began feverishly jerking off his shirt, careless of whether he woke her or not. The thought of simply holding her naked body close to him possessed him.

He hurled the shirt out on to the floor and during the brief couple of seconds that the curtains swung apart he thought he saw, in the dim starlight, her dark lashes lift. Then he was holding her close, stroking her supple back as he pressed her tightly into the contours of his body.

He held her in his arms, content for the moment with this physical contact. Then she gave a sleepy murmur and her arms curled up round his neck. He kissed her mouth and it was warm and soft, strengthening his desire to possess her. He had no thought now of her gentle birth, or her innocence. She had awoken urges that he had not realised he possessed. Gently, he rolled her on to her back and as his desire reached its climax and he thrust forward she seemed to wake, so that her quick gasp and cry of pain was sleep-blurred still.

When he lay still, sated and filled with love for his wife, he asked tenderly if he had hurt her and received her reassurance, timidly given.

'Before—I was afraid to offend you by brutish desire,' he said awkwardly. 'But your nakedness made me forget everything but lust.'

'It's no lust for a man to desire his wife,' Liza protested gladly. She nuzzled his neck softly, breathing into his ear, and he felt a renewed stab of longing. 'Why, to be woken from sleep to find oneself in the act of love is surely the most wonderful thing, Francis.'

'I was not over-eager? I know little of wooing, Liza.'

'You were perfect. And as to wooing, I know less, Francis.'

He felt quite different at her words. A man of the world, teaching his beautiful innocent girl how to enjoy love-play. She was his wife, and though she was young and well-born, she was woman enough to respond when the man she loved led the way. The man she loved! Sir Francis was sure now that she loved him, even as he worshipped her. No untried girl could have nestled in the arms of a man she did not love as Liza was nestling. Her breath was warm on his neck, and her hair flowed across his chest. He moved and she moved too, tucking herself closely against him. She raised her face and her lips brushed his.

Sir Francis remembered his first wife and felt vaguely guilty. But Mary had been nearly of an age with him—solid, comfortable, reliable. A good warm bed-mate, a good housewife, an excellent cook. When he had made love to her, she had been more complaisant than passionate; and she had never made him feel *special,* as he did now. She had come to him a virgin, to be sure. Yet bedding her had been for him an enjoyable exercise rather than the almost spiritual experience he had known with Liza.

She was a good girl, his Liza. She had waited patiently for him to choose the moment for their coming together. She had learnt her first lessons in his arms, and was offering her love and confidence as a child brings the first violets to its mother's knee. She responded to his touch, so that his hands could explore her beautiful, firm young body. In the morning I'll see her, he thought exultantly. His poor Mary had been an obedient wife but a shy one; she never removed all her clothes even in the warmest weather and he laughed aloud at the sudden realisation that though he had seen her in all the different stages of undress, he had never seen her naked.

But this little wife was young and eager to please him. He would wake first, and enjoy her with his early morning vigour. Then he'd pull back the bedclothes and feast his eyes on the pink-tipped breasts, the rounded curves and soft, dark hollows.

Marriage and bed suddenly seemed like a beautiful sort of game that they could both enjoy. He thought with wonder that he'd used the word 'pleasure' in connection with women, and never realised before what it could mean. He could only feel sorrow for the five days he had missed, by his ignorance and stupidity.

He felt her head grow suddenly heavy on his breast and knew that she slept again. But he lay awake a little while longer, savouring the knowledge that he had taken her maidenhead without losing her respect or affection even for a moment. If anything, he had gained from her loss. He allowed sleep to overtake him, knowing that his dreams would be sweet; that he would no longer fear himself inadequate in the company of beautiful women. One beautiful woman loved and trusted him. He asked no more.

★ ★ ★ ★

Elizabeth woke first in the morning. At some stage during their lovemaking they had changed places, and now the carelessly pulled bedcurtains through which Drake had hurled his shirt let the light shine on to her thick white lids, so that she woke and turned her head to look at her husband.

He lay relaxed in sleep, looking younger and more carefree than he did when you could see his eyes, sharp with responsibility and interest, their glance shrewd and calculating.

Elizabeth smiled softly to herself. It had been infamous, of course, to pretend sleep; especially since it was a trick she had heard Dorothy Howard boast of years before, when she had wanted a man who thought her too young for his bed.

'I was fourteen, too young to want to show him I desired him even as he desired me,' she had told the other girls. 'So one quiet afternoon in high summer I sat on the grass to pick daisies for a chain.' She had laughed wickedly. 'He sat beside me, his fingers trembling as he picked the flowers, and I knew what he was thinking of. So at last I lay back and feigned sleep, moving my body nearer to him as though in the depths of dreaming. He couldn't resist a chance to touch, and to him I seemed to respond in my sleep. So I seduced him, and to this day, no doubt, he thinks he seduced me.'

Elizabeth thought guiltily: Well, at least I only seduced my husband, and not some poor young man who would feel shame afterwards for his actions. She had guessed that Drake was reluctant to put his ardour to the test, but had wondered whether he felt scruples because of her youth, or because he doubted his own virility. But now she knew, and was satisfied that she had done the right thing. Left to himself, Heaven knew how long it might have taken him to make up his mind that she should be his wife in more than name. And she was aware that, for her, such waiting would have been a bad thing. A man and a woman who share a bed must be lovers, if both are normal. She believed that had she let Drake's feelings take their course, she must have come to the conclusion that there was something lacking in herself, so that when he *had* decided to make love to her she would have been nervous, withdrawn and cold.

She put out her hand and ran it gently through his thickly curling hair. He stirred and mumbled something, then his eyes opened in two gleaming slits and he pulled her close to him and smiled. It was a smile of pure delight, with no recollection of past difficulties to cloud his pleasure.

'Isabelle will be coming presently to wake us,' she warned him, but she yielded to his arms, knowing now that with women at least, his confidence was for show only. Though, at this rate, she thought with an inward smile, he'll have all the confidence he needs and more, for he is proving himself as able with a woman as he is with a ship.

'Oh, my master mariner,' she whispered, chuckling, and was rewarded by his answering laugh.

5

ALL SUMMER LONG

During that spring and summer, Elizabeth came to know many more things than the love of a husband. Many would-be mariners visited them, and came to appreciate Liza's unvarying calm and good humour, whether they came in state or unannounced. For Liza's part, she soon recognised that in a house so happily disorganised as theirs was likely to be, it was of the utmost importance that she should be on the best of terms with the servants, and that the servants themselves were the best available.

As spring began to merge into summer, Sir Francis told Liza that they would visit Buckland Abbey, where much work still needed doing, but where there was more room for them and their guests. Together, they rode out over Dartmoor, the sweetness of the grass and heather underfoot making a pleasant contrast to the salty tang of the sea.

'What do you think of it?' asked Sir Francis anxiously, as they breasted the slight rise and saw the Abbey and its outbuildings lying in a slight hollow below them.

Liza sighed with pleasure. The great house with its battlements, the crinkled golden tiles rusty with lichen, the small, arched windows and the mighty trees made a beautiful picture, and the parkland with its herds of deer reminded her sharply of her home in Somerset.

'It's magnificent,' she said softly. 'It's not hard to imagine that the monks still live here, tending the grapevines on the hill where their fruit is sheltered from the winds, to ripen in the sun; or toiling in the vegetable garden, or guiding the plough.'

Sir Francis snorted. 'Monks, thanks be to God, toil here no longer, if they ever did,' he said briskly. 'From what I've heard, most of the monks slept late, got others to work for them, and womanised. No, this is the cradle of the Grenvilles—or was, rather. Now, perhaps, it will be overrun by brats of our making.'

Children and religion, thought Liza crossly. She had not known the extent of her husband's Puritanism when they married, and she was lucky enough that though a deeply religious man he thought the Puritan ideas of plainness in dress and behaviour shockingly foolish. But he harboured a grudge against the Catholics, for to him Catholicism meant the Inquisition, and that, of course, meant Spain. He had lost many good friends to the cruel tortures of the friars of the Inquisition; and as a child, she knew, he and his family had been forced to flee from Crowndale because of his Protestant leanings. They had gone to Kent, where his father had begged the use of an old ship on the Medway as a dwelling for his wife and family.

As for children, she realised that every man wanted to leave something of himself behind him when he died. And in a way, she was luckier than most. Francis never allowed her to believe that she had not quickened with child through any fault of her own. The fault, he was sure, lay in him, because Mary, poor forgotten Mary, had been childless also.

But because of her youth and small frame, she sometimes thought crossly that he never really considered her a woman.

Rather, a delightful child, the daughter he had never been given, who kept house for him and wore beautiful clothes and delighted his friends with her ready wit and sympathetic ear. In bed, she was something else again—no fatherly thoughts towards me *there*, she thought with satisfaction. Bedding her was something special, for she was always eager to give him pleasure, knowing that bed was the only place that he had ever felt himself not complete master of every situation. And even as he took her in his arms, she knew that in a way he was asking for her; the fact that she gave joyously and without stint did not lessen his never-failing gentleness towards her. She was aware that once married, few women were mistress of their own bodies, to give or withhold favours as they chose. But Sir Francis had made it clear from the first that she could dictate, if she so wished, the terms of their lovemaking. The fact that she did not so wish made him, paradoxically, love and revere her more.

'Shall we go inside the house?' said Drake, and Liza nodded. The horses cantered down the slope and a stablehand ran up to take the animals as Drake dismounted and helped Liza from the

95

saddle. Then he led her by one hand into the cool darkness of the stone corridor behind the great front door, and into the huge room which had once been the church part of the Abbey. Now, the sun shone through the small paned windows on to an elaborately tiled floor, and the ceiling was elegantly moulded in plaster—shapes geometrical and severe and fantastically curved made the ceiling almost as interesting as the coloured tiles on the floor. The panelling was new and shone palely from the waxings it had been given by servants anxious to please their new mistress. Otherwise the great room was empty, save for the dancing dust motes in the sunbeams.

'I have done little furnishing, I thought it might please you to make this house beautiful whilst I'm at sea,' Sir Francis said diffidently, and was rewarded by Liza's little gasp of delight and the involuntary tightening of her small fingers round his hand.

After that, they passed through a bewildering array of rooms, all finely proportioned and well kept, but mostly, like the hall, unfurnished. On the ground floor, as they were going outside to see the stables and gardens, Drake showed Liza with simple pride a small chapel with just enough room for a simple altar and a half a dozen or so worshippers.

'You won't have to ride to the village, or into Plymouth to St Andrew's, to go to church when I'm at sea,' he told her. 'For we'll have a cleric visit the house for service once or twice a day, and any guests who wish may take advantage of his presence.'

But though Liza nodded, she scarcely heeded his words. Already, plans for the beautifying of this lovely building filled her head. She could see it was imposing enough for many of the rich and magnificent prizes that her husband kept in store in Plymouth, having no room for them in his town house. The barbaric silks and tapestries would not look out of place in these rooms—and Liza knew her taste to be beyond reproach. At a time when many of the nobles in England were making themselves ridiculous by the extravagance of their dress, Liza was comfortably aware of her own carefully chosen and unostentatious garments. To be sure, she wore enormous farthingales under her gown because that was the prevailing fashion. But she only did so when she was 'on show' as a guest or hostess, and not in the comfortable privacy of their home life. And even when dressed for company, her ruffs were not ridiculous cartwheels preventing her from turning her head, and her jewellery was adequate. She was one of the few women who did not hang half the jewellery in her possession upon her person on every available occasion, preferring the simplicity of a necklace, a jewelled girdle, perhaps, and one or two rings, rather than the hotch-potch of ill-assorted items worn by her contemporaries.

'This is the tithe barn of the old monks,' said Sir Francis, cutting across her thoughts. 'See, Liza, how they took from the poor people of Dartmoor to enrich their Abbey. The place could hold food for thousands—and probably did.'

They entered the great gloomy barn cautiously, squinting into the dusty dimness after the bright day outside. High overhead towered the great arched wooden beams, and now only a corner of the place was sufficient for the fruits garnered from the estate.

When they returned to Plymouth, Liza began, tentatively, to plan one of the rooms in her grand new house. But soon she was too busy with the delightful task of entertaining her husband's friends to have much time for pondering the respective qualities of satin or damask.

Into her wide living-room they swaggered, to talk of their voyage over the meal over which she and the cook had taken such care. Sometimes, as Martin Frobisher ate absently, talking all the while to Richard Hawkins, gesturing widely with a marinated chicken leg, Liza flinched and wondered whether they would notice if she set a nice dish of household refuse before them. Then they would suddenly turn to her, charming and appreciative smiles on their faces, and drink her health in the glowing red wine. At such times, she knew it *was* worthwhile; she was doing her part towards England's glory, though it might be a small one.

Often they strolled in her garden, plucking a sweet-smelling herb to tuck into a doublet and sniff as they picked their way over the stinking kennels in the streets back to their homes or lodgings. For with high summer, the fresh wind off the sea could not clear the lingering odours of rotting food and garbage in the streets. Drake himself, who appeared insensitive to the stench which seemed to Liza to turn the air blue, usually came back from a day at sea, trying the paces of a new longboat, and indignantly ordered a bonfire to be lit in the kennels. For a few days then, the streets were sweet again, but soon it was a case of burying one's nose in a posy of scented flowers or herbs, or sniffing at one's highly scented pomander, and scuttling quickly to one's destination.

Sometimes, Liza would think to herself: These are great men; I'm helping to make history. But such thoughts came rarely. Besides, she was unhappily conscious that beside the broad-shouldered, open-handed captains and courtiers, Sir Francis needed all his swagger and powerful personality. Some of the younger men, who regarded her husband with almost idolatrous worship, were struck by her beauty and would have tried their luck in seducing her had they not admired Sir Francis above all others.

Like any pretty girl, Liza gloried in her position as queen bee in this garden of glorious young men and hard-muscled, experienced older ones. And in the warmth of their open admiration she flourished, unfurling new petals of beauty that she had not known to attract and her duty to repel. She would have been less than human had she not, very occasionally, allowed her hand to be held and kissed at parting a fraction too long, so that the colour came to her cheeks; once or twice a conventional kiss of greeting had been full of suppressed ardour, and she had allowed her lips to soften instead of primming them together in righteous outrage.

Most of the men who were to sail in the autumn recognised these signs for what they were—a very young girl, newly married to an older man, trying her wings a very little, though she had no desire or intention of fluttering from the nest. But some wondered whether she saw too little of Sir Francis now that he was so busy with his fleet.

Liza learned to handle efficiently the situation where a handsome young man came to the house during the day knowing full well she would be alone except for the servants, intent on proving himself an attractive alternative to her husband. She became skilful at the task of disillusioning these young men, never hurting their self-esteem more than she could help, but nevertheless conveying the message unmistakably. The lady was not in need of any lover other than Drake!

Then, as summer turned towards autumn and outside her window little white puffs of cloud chased each other across the burning blue sky, something happened which speeded up the departure of the fleet in no uncertain fashion.

Liza's parlour was crowded with men who would sail with her husband. Sir Francis Knollys, the Queen's own cousin and a charming man; the Vice-Admiral of the Fleet, Martin Frobisher; Richard Hawkins; Edward Careless; the Fenner brothers and a crowd of others. There was a disturbance outside the door and two men strode into the room, hesitated, and made towards the hostess. They were Sir Philip Sidney and his close friend, Fulke Greville. There was a moment of startled silence, then a babble of talk and conjecture broke out. Philip, eyes sparkling and fair hair on end, kissed Liza quickly, squeezing her arms.

'Surprised, pretty one? I've decided to sail with your husband. To take the chance of death or glory by his side,' he declared, grinning at Liza's astonished face.

'Delighted, Sidney,' interposed Drake

quickly. 'Glad to have you with us. Here, sit down! Find the men a couple of chairs, lads.'

Fulke and Philip sat down eagerly and began to eat as though famished.

'Had to leave the Court pretty quickly,' Sidney explained through a mouthful of stewed mutton and button mushrooms. 'The Queen doesn't fancy me risking my person upon the high seas, far less dear old Greville here.' He laughed, and his blue eyes caught Liza's, full of outrageous amusement. 'Had to give her the slip, to tell you the truth. Left before dinner and rode like hell to reach Plymouth before she realises we're missing. Couldn't stop for a meal or a rest, just kept riding our horses out, changing them for fresh ones, and riding again.'

'You'll have been missed by now,' said Liza thoughtfully, remembering the Queen's eagle eye for a young man who had her favour.

'Oh, yes. Sure to be. But my sister Mary's a good girl. Told her to tell the Queen we had talked of Penshurst; business matters to attend to.' He pushed another generous spoonful of mushrooms into his mouth and said thickly, 'True, too. Wouldn't lead Mary into telling lies to the Queen. Told my little wife that I was feeling sore because the Queen wouldn't give me the governorship of Flushing, so *she'll* be in no trouble. Very likely, by the time the news of our whereabouts filters through to the Queen, we'll all be safe at sea.' He gulped down his mouthful and gave Drake a dazzling smile. 'I'll be no trouble, work as a sailor under your orders. Same for old Greville. Right, Fulke?'

'It's true enough, sir,' said Fulke Greville with obvious sincerity. 'We're not here on a wild-goose chase either, now that Sidney has been made Master of the Ordnance.'

'Quite,' Drake said, a trifly dryly. 'And no doubt you would do well in positions of command. But as sailors ...'

'Forget I'm Master of the Ordnance,' said Sidney grandly. 'I'll serve you as any ordinary seaman would.'

'Well, Master of the Ordnance or not, you're here now,' Martin Frobisher said calmly. 'Eat what you need, then we'd better find beds for you. Tomorrow you can be shown over the fleet.'

The evening was doubly entertaining for Sidney's presence, Liza thought. He brought a whiff of the Court, of gallantry and audacity, to men who had been long engaged on far more prosaic if more stimulating work. He was a good talker, too. He held his own end of the conversation well until the men began to talk of that other voyage, started in the *Pelican,* finished in the same ship rechristened the *Golden Hind.* Then he fell silent, his eager, hero-worshipping blue eyes going from face to face, his expressive features showing his every emotion.

Richard Hawkins, since he lived near by and had room enough, offered the two young men a bed, and they went off together in the early hours of the morning, when the party broke up.

Liza, stumbling upstairs quite giddy with tiredness, heard Francis say behind her, 'God, what will this mean? The Queen will never stand for it. She hates defiance—look how she kept poor Greville stewing here in Devon because she fancied him. Her pretty boys have to be near at hand; she can't bear to think of 'em on the loose, or in trouble.'

Liza began undressing. She had grown used to late nights and usually sent Isabelle off to bed early, knowing that Drake would assist her with difficult back fastenings.

Then Isabelle could be fresh for the morning and the pleasantly difficult task of choosing her dress for the day.

'Sir Philip isn't just one of the Queen's pretty boys,' she said reproachfully. 'Nor Fulke either. What will you do, Frank? Can you take them as mariners? Or will the Queen explode with fury and stop the whole enterprise?'

Drake, already stripped to a shirt and hose, said suddenly, 'Of course! I'll have to send a messenger to the Queen.'

'Oh, my darling, that seems so underhand. Couldn't you persuade Sidney to tell the Queen himself, or change his mind and go home?'

Drake, scrambling back into his clothes, shook his head. 'Impossible. He's got character and determination, that one, besides having the very devil of a temper when roused. He means well, but he's one who commands. The life of a sailor jumping to obey orders would soon pall and we'd be in trouble. However, if the Queen were to give her permission we'd have to make the best of it. Nothing must stop the fleet from sailing.'

Liza sighed but agreed, and tumbled into bed as Drake left the room and hurried

106

down the stairs in his usual impetuous fashion when there was work to be done. It was some time before he returned, but when he did he was happier.

'Great minds think alike, little one,' he said, slipping into bed beside her. 'One of the servants had a message from Knollys and another from Frobisher, suggesting we inform the Court as soon as possible. They each left a messenger, and a strong horse. So now three men have set out to find the Queen, to tell her of her favourite's truancy.'

The following day, Sidney's interest and enthusiasm were so great that Drake almost forgot his earlier strictures on the young man's character and felt a pang of regret that because of a woman's whim he would probably be denied this intelligent and likeable lad's company in his fleet. But not all Sidney's considerable charm was sufficient to banish the knowledge that to risk the Queen's displeasure was to risk losing permission to sail. That was what mattered.

'I shall captain the *Elizabeth Bonaventure*,' he told his uninvited guests as he showed them over the ships at anchor in Sutton Pool. 'There will be more than twenty ships in the fleet—two of them are owned by the Queen—but none is finer than the *Elizabeth Bonaventure*.'

'Did you name her for your pretty little wife, or for her Majesty?' asked Sidney idly, and Drake, laughing, replied, 'Would it be undiplomatic to say that I've never jumped aboard the Queen, but have enjoyed many voyages in my own little vessel?'

The men roared with laughter and Sidney said, 'Drake, Drake, you were never a diplomat. To us you may be your honest self, but to the Queen all men give their hearts with their allegiance—or such is the pretty concept of the moment. So she pleases you, the little Sydenham?'

'She pleases me,' Drake said softly, his eyes glowing with reminiscence, and Sidney suddenly remembered that dear Fulke had once been in love with the little Sydenham, and wriggled uncomfortably.

But during the laughter, Fulke had wandered off and was gazing at the clean lines of the ship which towered above him. He was thinking, however, of Liza. She had changed, certainly. Marriage had softened her, yet it had given her self-confidence. Her beauty now was a glowing thing, lit by happiness, lovely to behold. He had felt the previous evening when he stood by her that he was warmed by her flame, and he had luxuriated in that warmth. But when Drake had spoken of voyaging in the little Sydenham it seemed from the stab of pain that cut at his heart that admiring her was not enough. He had thought himself free from the itch of desire for her; now he realised that it had never really left him and that the sight of her and the words of her husband which spoke of the ultimate intimacy made him feel like a hungry man denied food.

Once I held her in my arms and kissed her mouth, he thought. But with such reverence and respect! He'd been a fool. Why, he could give Drake a good fifteen years and he had the Court polish that Drake lacked. Then he shrugged, and turned back to his two companions. What use was it crying over an *affaire* he had never had the courage to push to its conclusion? He realised that Drake was speaking to them both and dragged his mind back to the present: the tall ships and the waves slapping the sides of the quay.

'Come to a banquet in my house—not the house in Plymouth, but out at Buckland

Abbey. It's not fully furnished yet—I'm leaving that for my Liza to do whilst I'm at sea. But it's still a fine place, and I've sent servants and cooks to prepare for us. I've invited several prominent townsfolk who would like to meet you both, the captains and commanders of the expedition, and some neighbours and friends. But now, if you'll forgive me, I must speak to the men working on the victualling.'

And whilst the two young courtiers swaggered round the town, thinking themselves pretty good fellows to have given the Queen the slip so that they could risk their lives with Drake, Drake himself was cooking up a further plan.

'I can't be easy as to what the Queen means to do,' he muttered to Frobisher below the noise of the carpenters banging and sawing and making all good. 'Suppose the messenger comes back forbidding us to set sail at all, until the Queen has dealt with Sidney? Suppose that she forbids me to take him, and he refuses to leave? Good God, Martin, suppose she thinks I'm responsible (for she must know Sidney and I are friends) and forbids *me* to sail? *Me*, to whom this expedition means everything!'

The horror and despair at such a thought

written plainly on his shrewd, self-reliant face was almost comical, and Frobisher laughed. 'God man, you're not to blame for a lively lad wanting to live a normal life instead of being mewed up at Court. How could she, with justice, keep you at home?'

'Justice? What do women know of justice, when they're annoyed?' grumbled Drake. 'By God, Frobisher, but your Yorkshire common sense has done me good. I've had an idea.'

His face lit up suddenly, and a dimple appeared in one tanned cheek. But he would not tell Frobisher more. Bidding his friend a hurried goodbye, he disappeared into the nearest tavern with a haste which made even the phlegmatic Frobisher raise his brows, knowing Drake to be an abstemious man.

However, it was not until later that day that Frobisher was able to put two and two together and draw his own conclusions regarding Drake's sudden and unusual tavern visit.

Liza and her servants had worked feverishly all day at Buckland Abbey, preparing the great banquet for their guests. Stools and tables had been brought out from their storage places and set up in the great hall; and the kitchen fires blazed forth, roasting meats and pies, so that the cooks worked stripped to the waist, and the scullions turning the spits called constantly for ale.

Liza bustled round, supervising the arrangement of the furniture, filling great bowls with the gaudy blossoms of late summer, and answering the anguished questions put to her by the overworked servants.

After much thought, she had decided that as food and drink would probably flow in the most literal sense, it would be a wise precaution to cover the beautiful floor tiles with strewing herbs, so she and Isabelle raided the tithe barn and sent out a bevy of village girls to gather meadowsweet. Then she hurried upstairs to the room she and Sir Francis would share later that evening. Now it was a woman's boudoir, though, with a tub of water for her to bath in, and clothes laid out on the bed.

Quickly, she and Isabelle stripped off her sensible working gown and Isabelle helped her young mistress into the luke-warm bathwater. Liza shivered ecstatically as the cool liquid engulfed her overheated body and washed gently round her waist. Isabelle handed her scented soap and they talked quietly as Liza slowly lathered herself and then slid under the water again, to emerge reluctantly at Isabelle's reminder that soon her guests would begin to arrive.

'The gown is a new one, milady,' Isabelle reminded her. 'The bodice will be stiff and the fastenings difficult. Best give ourselves plenty of time.'

'Yes, pale pink silk embroidered with wild white roses,' said Liza with some satisfaction. 'When I greet our guests, Belle, I bet they think I've spent the day strolling in the grounds or lying on my bed, and not in cooking their supper!'

'You rather fancy yourself as a Somerset rose, don't you, milady?' said Belle slyly, smiling at the younger girl affectionately.

'Well, it is true that pink suits me,' said Liza, parrying the question. 'I say, Belle, you were right about the bodice! It feels as though someone has fashioned it out of good old English oak.'

The two girls wrestled with the ornate clothes. The shift, crisp from its recent laundering, had a low, plain neck, and when the bodice was struggled into, the full bishop's sleeves adjusted and the gown lowered carefully into place, Liza looked with frank anxiety down at her white bosom.

'This bodice is awfully low-cut, Belle,' she said doubtfully. 'And it's so stiff that it has forced my breasts half out at the top. Have we no high-necked shift, or a partlet, perhaps?'

'You bade me bring your new outfit, and so I have, down to the white slippers with pink bows,' said Isabelle. 'But not another garment did I pack. Now why are you worrying? A bodice low-cut is no uncommon thing at Court, and this banquet is in Sir Philip's honour, isn't it? Well, he's newly come from Court—he'll see nothing strange in your bodice.'

'It's not what's *in* my bodice that worries me,' said Liza fretfully, 'but what is out of it.' She moved over to the mirror and gave a shriek.

'God in Heaven, Belle, it's indecent! Oh, oh, when I lift my arms I feel certain my bosom will pop out at the top! Can't you *do* something?'

'Your jewels!' cried Isabelle, suddenly remembering. 'I didn't know which necklaces and rings you would want, so I brought the lot. If you wear lots and lots of beads, and strings of pearls and so on, you can cover most of your bosom.'

'I'm not going downstairs festooned in a queen's ransom,' protested Liza. 'But you're right, Belle, there must be jewellery there that would make me look less naked.'

Feverishly the two young women searched until they found the most ornate and concealing necklace of all. It was a barbaric-looking gold collar wrought in soft metal, from which hung quantities of gold leaves, pearl droplets and tiny emerald chips. Danging from the centre, as a sort of pendant, was a large ruby, carved in the likeness of a rose.

'I look like an Indian savage queen, but it will have to do,' said Liza heavily, gazing at her reflection. 'Oh, Belle, wouldn't it just have to happen when I particularly wanted to look my best? Some of the men will bring their wives, who'll think I'm a fast, loose-living creature with no dress sense.'

'Not in that necklace, they won't,' said Isabelle grimly. 'Their eyes will be too busy calculating the cost to worry overmuch whether your dress is cut too low. Now stop moaning, do, Miss, and let me get at your hair.'

In honour of the occasion, she piled Liza's hair on top of her head and kept it in place with a gold fillet shaped in the likeness of a garland of flowers.

'You look lovely, milady,' she said earnestly, then, 'Gracious, what's that noise in the hall?'

'The guests!' shrieked Liza, making for the door like a startled hare. 'Oh, Belle, and I not there to greet them.' She reached the head of the stairs before remembering her dignity and slowing her pace to a walk. She could feel her heart bumping as she descended the stairs and wondered if her foolish impetuosity had uncovered any more bosom, but a quick peep proved her fears to be groundless.

Nevertheless, her *décolletage* occupied a good half of her mind throughout the banquet, so that she did not notice her husband's rather strained joviality, or the quizzical glances Martin Frobisher kept throwing in his direction.

One of the distinguished company was Sir William Courtenay with his wife, yet another Elizabeth. Though Lady Elizabeth Courtenay was great with child, she was dressed in all the tricks and bobbery imaginable, and Liza could only be glad that there was scarcely time for a brief introduction before she passed on to greet her next guests, for to admire the other woman's gown would have been impossible. When they sat down to eat, Liza found herself with William Courtenay sitting beside her, whilst his wife was several places further down the board. She noticed as he smiled his remembered, rakish smile that he eyed her as hotly as though he knew nothing of the tight-lipped woman who was to bear his child.

'Well met, little Sydenham,' he said softly, under cover of the general conversation. 'What a delightful gown! And your necklace is charming, quite charming.'

Liza, confused, managed to keep her countenance, though she could not prevent a slight, betraying warmth rising to her cheeks.

'I'm no longer the little Sydenham, sir,' she said coolly. 'I'm Lady Elizabeth Drake. You would do well to remember it.'

'You're right, of course,' agreed Courtenay smoothly. 'And you would do well to remember that when you lean forward like that, your necklace does not do its work.'

Liza straightened abruptly and felt the

rose-ruby slip into the cleft between her breasts.

'How I would love to be your little pendant,' her tormentor continued in a caressing undertone. 'To nestle in such a spot would be happiness indeed! What does Sir Francis think of your gown?'

As he spoke, he placed a hand below the table firmly on Liza's thigh. Liza felt her face go hot. He was unspeakable, really he was. But what could she do? The hand was moving upward now, and never had Liza felt more grateful to farthingales, for she thought his touch could distinguish little beneath such a formidable garment. She looked at him. He was doing it to annoy and disturb, obviously. The infuriating thing was that he was succeeding. She suddenly felt not only annoyed and disturbed, but very young and vulnerable.

She did not know whether to be glad or sorry that they were in the midst of a large gathering. Whilst she was in reality safe enough, he could embarrass her unhindered, for she dared not slap his face. Then a thought came to her, and she picked up the small Italian fork she used to dispense the contents of the dish in front of her. Smiling pleasantly, she leaned forward provocatively and felt his hand stiffen as his eyes fell on her rounded young breasts.

It was to his credit that he did not even give vent to the smallest yelp when she pushed the fork into the back of his hand with all her strength—he removed it pretty sharply though, and Liza watched with gentle malice as his face purpled in an endeavour to contain the shout that he must have longed to give.

Then they were both laughing, and he was saying, 'I should have learned my lesson years ago. My, you were a wildcat then, you're five times as bad now!'

'So are you,' retorted Liza. 'It was ungentlemanly to remark on my gown, let alone anything else. I'm sure you realised as soon as we sat down that I felt foolish with such a neckline.'

'Neckline, do you call it? More like a waistline,' he teased. 'But, really, child, your necklace gave away your secret—to anyone who knows you well, that is. I've never seen you flaunting a great gold collar covered in spangles, so I guessed at once you were using it to hide your—er—low neckline. Now may I make my peace, and apologise?'

'Of course. And I'm sorry about the fork,' said Liza at once. She added with a sudden giggle, 'Goodness, look at it! The prongs are bent. You must have skin like leather.'

He was about to reply when a messenger came into the room and approached Sir Francis. He was very dishevelled and looked both annoyed and embarrassed. Liza, thinking of her recent predicament, felt sorry for him and gave him an encouraging smile.

He addressed Sir Francis without preamble, however.

'Sir, I have come from London, on urgent business for her Majesty the Queen. I've brought three messages. One was to the Mayor of Plymouth and is delivered. The others are for you and Sir Philip Sidney.' He handed a folded parchment to Sir Francis and said stiffly, 'I regret that the seals are broken, sir. But a few miles outside Plymouth I was set upon by four ugly customers armed with cudgels. They took my despatches from me, but having read them, returned them unharmed, if dirty. Sir, there's something odd afoot, for one of them said jestingly, "You should at least give us the price of a drink," and another cut in sharply, "Quiet, man! That was no part of the bargain." Yet they were ugly rogues, and I thought myself lucky to escape with my life, let alone my purse and my despatches.'

Drake and Sidney opened their missives almost simultaneously, and Liza saw with some distress the excitement and animation drain from Sir Philip's face.

'No need to tell me, Sir Francis,' he said sadly. 'Forbids you to take me on the voyage, does she not? Same here. Offers me the Governorship of Flushing to sweeten the dose, though, so I shan't be idle. I'd like to know how she found out where I'd gone so damned quickly, nevertheless.'

'Probably guessed, Sidney,' remarked Frobisher, and Sir William Courtenay agreed with a grin. 'Devilish clever at guessing, the Queen,' he confirmed, glancing sideways at Liza. 'Did a very neat bit of guessing once at my expense which sent me scuttling down to Devon.'

'She must have known you were hot to join the fleet, Phil,' said Drake somewhat uncomfortably. 'You said yourself you'd been talking of it for months. She's a canny one, the Queen.'

'What about the despatch despoilers who let their victim and his letter carry on undisturbed?' asked someone else, and Drake said with an attempt at nonchalance, 'Probably moon-men in search of a purse of gold. Thought there might be something in the letters, perhaps, that they might use for blackmail. But never mind them, now's the time to drink up, and tell a tale or two round the table, for tomorrow our guests must leave us.'

It was late at night, therefore, before the guests, some pot-flown with wine, others over-excited at the thought of the coming adventure, made for the chambers the servants had hurriedly got ready for them. Liza and Francis stripped and tumbled into bed, both physically and mentally exhausted by their day.

'Why did you arrange for the messenger to be waylaid?' Liza said suddenly in a conversational tone.

Drake yawned elaborately, and said, 'What? What? Go to sleep, little one. Morning will come soon enough.'

Liza rolled over and, burying her fingers in her husband's tousled locks, said fiercely, 'Tell me, or I'll pull, I swear it.'

'Nothing to tell, my pretty—ouch, don't!'

'Then tell. Come, Frank, to one who knows you it was obvious that you knew more than you cared to admit about those "rogues" as the messenger called them. Come to think of it, who else would know or could know? It was you who sent the first message to the Queen, after all.'

'Sly little puss. No, don't pull my hair out by the roots, I'm going to tell you so that I can get some rest. I got worried this morning, in case the Queen decided the whole mission was a mistake. So I persuaded four of my fellows—no rogues, but honest seamen every one—to waylay the messenger from London and read the despatches. If they contained messages to the effect that we were not to sail, the letters were to be destroyed and we would be off on the morning tide, ready or not. However, if they merely recalled Sir Philip, or even gave permission for him and Greville to stay, then they were to be given back to the messenger for delivery. Neat, don't you think?'

'Utterly unscrupulous and dreadful,' said Liza with a giggle. 'Who else knows, apart from your four lily-white sailors of course?'

'Frobisher may guess,' Drake said cautiously. 'Liza, I swear if you *do* pull my hair

I'll teach you a lesson you won't forget in a hurry. You asked for the truth and you've got it. Now be a good little wife and go to sleep. We've a hard day ahead of us tomorrow; you'll be cleaning up here and I'll be badgering the carpenters to make the best speed they may so that we can be off.'

'I'm not tired now, your story has woken me up,' protested Liza in an injured voice. 'Aren't you going to make love to me?'

'God save me from a vigorous young wife,' said Drake with a groan. 'No, I'm not! Go to sleep, you hussy!'

Liza gave a chuckle which turned into a yawn. 'Fortunately for you, I'm tired, too. Otherwise you wouldn't be allowed to turn your back on me and sleep when I'm feeling affectionate,' she said. 'And just remember when you wake up all keen and lively in the morning that *I* shall have a hard day ahead of me, and be in no mood for romping.'

Sir Francis heaved himself over in the bed and took Liza tenderly in his arms. 'Best of wives, you shall want for nothing, but tonight ...' he said, his voice already thickened with sleep.

Liza responded to his hug and said

comfortingly. 'Hush, my darling. Sleep this night at least. I mustn't tease you. Sleep.'

But she might as well have saved her breath, she thought, for the only reply she got was a small, throaty snore.

6

LEFT BEHIND

Once Sidney and Greville had departed for London, a frenzy seized the men to get the ships victualled and ready for departure. Not only Drake, but most of the officers, were secretly fearful that the Queen would suddenly change her notoriously capricious mind, and decide they could not be allowed to leave.

Liza thought she had never worked so hard. Even with the many hands ready and willing to help him, Drake depended on her in many small ways. It was Liza who found the merchant willing to sell them a supply of fresh oranges and lemons; according to Sir Francis, it was Liza's pleading smile and persuasive tongue that decided the merchant to sell them his entire cargo, at a cheaper rate than he could have got had he sold his fruits in the market.

Ever active, the men sweated with

renewed vigour at the thought of possible cancellation of their voyage; and Liza found herself worrying, too.

It was not, of course, that she wanted Sir Francis to leave her. But she had realised long ago, when he had first made her the object of his attention, that whilst life at home could be happy for him, it was only made so against the violent contrast of his maritime adventures. So she told herself firmly that, kept ashore, he might grow tired of her; but, between voyages, their married life could be a delicious honeymoon, to be enjoyed to the full and recalled with pleasure when they were parted once more by his job—the only mistress with whom she would ever have to compete.

In spite of their most frantic efforts, however, Drake decided to leave before the ships were properly victualled. With tears in her eyes, Liza stood by the harbour as the trumpets brayed to the men to leave the tavern and take up their duties aboard ship. Beside her, a pile of carefully boxed 'poor john', as dried Newfoundland fish was called, bore mute witness to the haste of their departure, for the crews often had to rely upon hardtack, dried fish, and the murky water in the bottom of the barrels before they had a chance to revictual the vessels.

'Goodbye, my darling. Take good care of yourself, and enjoy making Buckland beautiful, as only you can do,' Drake said, kissing Liza tenderly.

'Goodbye, my love. May your voyage prosper, and may God keep you,' said Liza carefully, staring hard at the cobbled quay and trying to keep her countenance. Then, when he took her in his arms, she burst out, 'Oh, Sir Francis, how I love you! Come back to me, that's all I ask.' She gave a watery sniff. 'Don't take risks,' she finished foolishly, blinking back the tears that wanted to fall.

Drake squeezed her shoulders, kissed her again, and was gone. Soon she could see him, busy aboard the *Elizabeth Bonaventure*, shouting orders, inspecting last-minute storage, trying out tackle. Men swarmed like ants in the rigging, setting the sails to catch the faint breeze of autumn. Occasionally, Drake cast his eye at Liza, standing on the quayside, her kerchief fluttering a last farewell. But it was mainly to gauge how far they had in fact travelled, for once on board his ship it was as though he had entered a different world.

Liza stood watching until the ships were small in the distance. Her legs ached, and her eyes hurt from straining against the sunlight to see the white patches of sail. Suddenly, it seemed, they slipped over the rim of the world and were gone, leaving the ocean calm and blue once more. A virgin sea, with no vessel sailing precariously across its mysterious depths.

Liza moved then. She turned, and saw she was alone. The other women who had come to bid their husbands farewell had left when the ships were too far away for individual faces to be picked out. But Liza was new to the business of seeing one's husband go away, into danger, without her. She hugged her big cloak round her and shivered. How quiet it was! Who could believe that Sutton Pool could be so empty and silent? For months, Plymouth had echoed and re-echoed to the sounds of ships and men. Even at night there had been no silence, for the wind sang in the rigging and timbers creaked and groaned.

But now, only the seagulls mewed their solitary lament. Only Liza's soft footfall sounded on the cobbles. She picked her way home up streets quiet with the hush of early evening. The cheering townspeople had gone indoors now, to eat a meal and talk of the recent excitement.

It was still warm enough for many windows to be open, and Liza caught the murmurs of conversation from families sitting at their tables. Shrill-voiced children being hushed, a father delivering an omnipotent opinion, a mother's harsh call to the serving wench to hurry. She picked her way across the kennel, nostrils wrinkling, and looked at her own house. Tall and beautiful, its candles lit so that the window glass gleamed an inviting red-gold. But empty.

For a moment Liza thought wildly of running away. Running anywhere, to be away from the home that had meant so much and now suddenly meant nothing at all. She could get a horse saddled and go home to visit her parents at Combe Sydenham. She could go to Court and visit the friends she had made when she was a maid of honour.

Then the front door opened and Isabelle stood there, peering out into the fast-thickening dusk, an anxious frown on her smooth forehead.

'Goodness, milady, we began to wonder if you'd gone a-sailing with Sir Francis after all,' she said reproachfully. She came down the steps, holding out her hand to Liza. 'Come now, the cook has prepared a delicious meal for you. We thought you'd feel lonely, perhaps, with Sir Francis gone.'

Liza gave Isabelle a piteous look, her dark eyes swimming with tears. 'Oh, Belle, I *am* lonely,' she said, her voice breaking. 'I knew he would go, of course, but I never let myself think about what I would do when he had left. And it's not only Sir Francis; the whole world seemed to go away with the ships. But I have *you,* and we'll find plenty to occupy us once the shock of the fleet leaving is over, won't we?'

'Of course we will,' said Isabelle soothingly, leading her mistress into the parlour and taking the cloak from her shoulders. 'Plymouth will seem quiet for a day or two, no doubt, but it will soon become itself again. And others are suffering from separation beside yourself, you know. Many a fine lady will weep into her pillow tonight and spend hours on her knees, praying for her man. Now sit down, Lady Liza, and eat the cook's dish of trout—it's one of your favourites, which is why he prepared it specially.'

Then Liza really did cry. Like a child, she knuckled her eyes, giving loud wailing sobs and saying between them, 'They had to leave the "poor john" behind them on the quay, Belle. I may have trout, but their fish is left behind at Sutton Pool. Oh, Belle, my poor Francis, what will *he* be eating tonight?'

'Why, the good fresh food we packed and stowed in his cabin aboard the *Elizabeth Bonaventure,* of course,' said Isabelle bracingly. 'It will last for a week at least—and by then he may have found a friendly harbour where he can revictual. As for drink, the wine will glow in his glass as it glows in yours. Now don't be foolish, milady, for you'll know real worry one of these days, so don't make yourself miserable without cause. Eat your food, like a good girl.'

The 'good girl' slumped in her seat and began to pick at the trout. But she had eaten nothing all day and soon her naturally healthy appetite was aroused. She began eating with gusto, suggesting different plans for the days to come.

'We must furnish the great house at Buckland; Sir Francis will expect *that* to be completed by the time he returns,' Liza said, through a mouthful of fish. 'Goodness knows, Belle, we have materials enough to do the job well, and willing hands to help us. If we choose to go to London then, Sir Francis has made arrangements for lodgings to be put at our disposal. But we won't leave Devon for long, because he may well find some means of sending despatches home, and will include letters for me, perhaps.'

'To be sure,' said Belle bracingly. 'When shall we set off for Buckland Abbey then, milady? For you'll want to live there whilst you make everything as it should be.'

Her eyes shone, envisaging not only the linen cupboards to be filled with freshly laundered sheets and starched tablecloths, but at the thought of being with a number of other servants all the time, for in Plymouth the servants, though both friendly and efficient, had to be lodged in a small cottage at the end of the garden, and extra labour brought in when occasion demanded. Belle herself slept in Liza's dressing-room, amongst the gowns and kirtles and piles of smocks and shifts. But in the Abbey, where space was to be had in plenty, all the servants would sleep on the premises, in the vast attics. The women would probably be in several dormitories and the men in others, but the higher servants would probably have a place of their own.

'You will want to hire extra help,' Isabelle said thoughtfully. She had several admirers in Plymouth, but one she would have liked to know better. He was a carpenter, and a good one too, who had worked on the ships being built in Sutton Pool and was also at work at the moment carving the newel posts of a house in New Street for Captain Wynter's wife and family. She guessed that there would be a good deal of work for a carpenter at Buckland. But her handsome Mark could wait for now. She would speak to him, and see if he would like to work at the Abbey.

That night, as she brushed and braided Liza's long hair before putting her mistress to bed, she eyed her own reflection covertly in the round mirror. Thick, golden brown hair parted neatly in the centre and kept under her cap with the pretty combs that Lady Liza had given her. A creamy golden skin dusted with freckles, and fresh red lips. She shifted her attention back to the braids which she was pinning into place on Liza's head. Yes, she would certainly get Mark Pennick to take the job. She would smile, and her eyes would tell the rest.

'You look like a cat that's got at the cream, Belle,' said Liza, turning and surveying the maid with an interested stare. 'What can have happened today, when all the mariners who tried to take liberties with you behind the lavender bushes or on the rough grass on the Hoe have gone to sea? Not met someone else already, have you?'

Bella sniffed scornfully. 'Most of 'em wanted to tumble me because they couldn't have you,' she said. 'These gentlemen, they're all the same. Eye a pretty lady until they're tickled with desire for her, then notice the comely serving wench and try to take liberties. I'd rather lie with a decent man of my own class who would wed me if he got me with child, than one of the fine gentlemen who would take his pleasure and leave me a-crying.'

'None of them would do such a thing,' protested Liza, but her face was lively with curiosity. 'Tell me, Belle, for we've

135

no secrets from each other. Which of the fine Court gentlemen did you lie with?'

Belle laughed. 'Not your own husband, for he has his heart's desire,' she said. 'But before he took his sour-faced wife home, one gentleman at the banquet at Buckland had taken his pleasure with me.'

Liza stared, all curiosity now, an enormous question mark.

'Oh, Belle, who was it, you dreadful girl? Do tell me, or I'll box your ears!'

Belle laughed again. 'His hair curls, and his skin is brown, for he has been to sea with Sir Walter Ralegh and served under him in Ireland,' she said provocatively. 'His body is lean and muscular and he lay in my arms afterwards and swore that I'd satisfied the appetite you'd roused in him, though he said he'd have you one day, despite you sticking him like a pig with the serving fork.'

'Courtenay?' gasped Liza. 'Well, you've got yourself a handful there, my girl. Did he recall you from our days at Court, I wonder? Do you remember the day he tried to rape me in a wood, and Fulke Greville brought me back to you to be comforted?'

'I was just a woman,' said Belle

comfortably. 'Of course, it wouldn't have occurred to Sir William that to me he was just a man. Satisfying my desire for another, even as I satisfied him. So no doubt he is full of conceit at having seduced your own personal maid, practically under your nose, too—with that sharp-faced wife of his close at hand.'

'When did he manage it? When?' said Liza, full of astonishment that such a thing could have happened on that evening which had been so full of surprises.

'Why, when else than after the messenger had left, and Sir Francis bade everyone forget the incident and fill up their glasses?' said Belle, giggling. 'He saw me ready to go to your side in case there was bad news and left his place as soon as he could, which was speedily filled by others wanting to be near you and Sir Francis. He gave me a cuddle in the shadows, then pulled me out of the hall into the little parlour next door. I was frightened that we'd be discovered, but I soon forgot to be afraid.' She laughed again, at the expression of awe on Liza's face. 'Go on, milady, don't tell me I'm no better than I ought to be! Poor man, fancy being married to that shrew, and her so great with child and so sharp that he can no more get near her than he can play off his games with their serving wenches.'

Liza laughed reluctantly, then more openly. 'Oh, Belle, you are dreadful. We'd better get you married before you disgrace us all. Now go off to bed and pray for forgiveness. I'll fall asleep counting sheets, and the cost of strewing rushes. Goodnight, dear Belle.'

★ ★ ★ ★

Yet, despite her conviction that a little hard work would see the Abbey looking just as it should, Liza found that Belle had been nearer the truth than herself. They had moved their supply of materials and some furniture to the Abbey, and found to Liza's annoyance it was like filling a pond with a small bucket. The principal bedchambers were large and empty—empty even of a bed! On the night of the banquet, most of the guests had been content with straw pallets, but now things must be put to rights. Not one carpenter, but several, were therefore employed. Liza decided not to travel to London until after the Christmas and New Year festivities were over, though she had to send a messenger to the city with a New Year gift for the Queen which Sir Francis had left with her, to pass on at the appropriate time to that other Elizabeth.

Then, at Christmas, she had her first letter from Sir Francis. It was brought to the Plymouth house by a sailor and carried to her at the Abbey by a footman, left behind to see that all was in order at the town house.

'My goodness, to think how I cried when they left without taking the "poor john" aboard their vessels,' Liza said to Belle. 'Yet Sir Francis says that a few days out of harbour, they met a Spanish ship carrying a cargo of that same fish, and relieved her of it. Then they began to run short of necessities in Vigo Bay, so they landed at some place called Bayona. He doesn't say much about that visit, except I will not be surprised to hear that there was Spanish treachery, but that in the end they were richer for it.'

'Sir Francis can turn most things to his advantage,' said Belle, with a smile. 'Where is the letter from, milady?'

'Santiago. They have taken the city and are going to ransom it or burn it to the ground. Sir Francis thinks the governor will pay the money. He is obviously in good spirits, despite the fact that he thinks they missed the Spanish treasure fleet. He doesn't say they found anything much in Santiago, but his letter has a sort of smirk which makes me wonder.'

'A letter with a smirk! Oh, milady!' protested Belle, laughing.

'Well, anyway, he's cheerful,' said Liza, scanning the letter again. 'Who is coming to our Christmas banquet, Belle? Are there any of his shipmates who might be interested in this letter, or did they all sail with him?'

'You haven't asked the Courtenays to any part of the festivities, have you?' said Belle slyly. 'Sir William is a bit of an adventurer himself and would be interested, of course.'

'What would your handsome carpenter say if I hinted that you wanted another tumble with Sir William, Belle, dear? I couldn't have him in the house, it wouldn't be fair to you,' Liza said with a grin.

'You're probably right not to ask him actually,' conceded Belle. 'He's a handsome man, and very set on you, milady. Your husband has been absent many weeks now—the rogue would undoubtedly try to warm your bed.'

'I'll warm your bottom if you make remarks like that,' snapped Liza. 'I have no intention of being unfaithful to Sir Francis, not even if he's away six months!'

'And I've no intention of being unfaithful to Mark, so we shouldn't talk about Sir William. I'm sorry, milady,' said Belle with genuine repentance. She watched the angry colour gradually fade from Liza's cheeks and wondered how much it meant to her mistress to be without a man.

Happily warm-hearted herself, with the comfortable assurance that what she gave to one man she was not keeping from another, Belle had been satisfied to dispense her favours where she chose, though never lightly. Now that she was sure of her love for Mark, however, she had no need of other men. They were to be married in the spring, and Belle knew without having to think about it, that once the knot was tied, no other man would try to steal a kiss behind the kitchen door, or fumble her breasts in the empty stillroom. But suppose Mark were to go a-voyaging, as Liza's husband had? Suppose, next time, Mark, too, was waving to her from the deck of a ship? Would she be able to ignore the lure of a handsome man? Could she lay in her lonely bed, night after night, when comfort and company were to be had for the asking?

She sighed. 'The new bed of inlaid marquetry for the bedroom we're working on now is almost ready,' she ventured. 'Shall we go and see whether the woods blend in with the general colour scheme?'

'I suppose so,' Liza said forlornly. 'It's better than sitting here, wondering about Sir Francis. I'll tell you what, Belle, when we get back let's hang the cloth of gold tapestries in the banqueting hall. We won't leave them up, of course, but we could get the general idea of how the room will look. I like the big, draw-leaf table your betrothed has made; it's strong and handsome, but light enough to be easily moved, and when the leaves are both out it will seat an amazing number of guests.'

'It is nice—and very modern,' agreed Belle. 'We'd better remind the gardeners about the yule log—to haul it right up to the hearth tonight so that it will be dry and ready for lighting tomorrow. Mark and some of the other workers can sleep by it to make sure it doesn't catch fire too soon!'

They wandered off, Liza happier because she had received Sir Francis' letter, yet sad because of his obvious enjoyment so that he only mentioned in passing how he missed her.

I have nothing to do but miss him, she thought, and then scolded herself fiercely. She had plenty to do. It was just that most of the things she did seemed purposeless with Sir Francis far away, unable to praise her for the improvements she was making on his new home.

7

LIVELY HOMECOMING

'He's home, he's home, he's back in England,' carolled Liza, darting into the passageway and seizing Isabelle by the arm. 'Here I am, determined to be on the quay to meet him, and for the first time anyone seems able to remember they had landed, not at Plymouth, but at Portsmouth! Of course, probably Frobisher thought it handier for London, and Carleill—who commanded the soldiery—must have agreed. But, oh, Belle, he's home, and safe. These past ten months have seemed like ten years, but now we can pack our gear and make all haste to London! He will have to report to the Queen, so we will go to lodgings in Broad Street and meet there.'

'Oh. Well, I'm very glad, I'm sure, milady. Will I leave my husband here, then, working at Buckland still?'

'Belle, Belle, don't be so greedy! I've been without *my* husband for ten months.

I don't suppose it will be long before we return to Plymouth. Now come and help me pack.'

'You've been ready any time this past four months,' protested Isabelle, laughing, as they made their way up the circular staircase of the Plymouth house. 'All I have to do is crate up a few garments which have lately been laundered. Does Sir Francis say how the expedition went?'

'Not really. But he has gifts for me.' She reached the top stair and spun round on the landing so that her wide skirts almost touched the walls and sent a young gale blowing into Isabelle's face. 'The best gift is himself,' she said proudly. 'And I shall be so happy to assure him that I've looked at no man with desire since he left us, all those months ago.'

★ ★ ★ ★

So when Sir Francis got to the comfortable lodgings he had hired after his interview with the Queen, he found the place bustling with servants and a girl with glowing eyes waiting to throw herself into his arms.

'Oh, my love,' she gasped, elated by his shout of joy and his strong hug. 'It's so wonderful to see you! As we rode up from Plymouth all England seemed to be singing your praises. Folk said that you'd not captured much in the way of treasure, but had done great harm to those wicked Spaniards, and had lost few men.'

'We lost many,' Drake contradicted her sadly. 'Some of our best men perished, though it was through sickness and not in warfare. Some disease we picked up at the Cape Verde Islands. It went through the fleet like wildfire and must have killed hundreds.'

'I'm terribly sorry, Frank,' said Liza, knowing that her husband set greater store by his men's lives than anything. 'Did I know any of the dead?'

'Tom Moone, Fortescue, Bigges and Grenville. And that's not the half, love.'

'I know how you have grieved and it grieves *me*, too,' said Liza in a small voice. 'But, oh, Frank, thank God you're safe! I've prayed for your life and well being, but so did the wives of those other good men. How is Frobisher? I know *he's* alive.'

'Yes, and kicking,' said Drake with a chuckle. 'But you know our Yorkshireman. He'll be back to his native county after this for a short rest before his next engagement.

He's a good man with ships, though there's little love lost between him and his men. They say he's an unlucky captain, you know—well, I can see their point—and he treats 'em rough. For myself, I respect my men and they me. Dandified courtiers can turn up their noses and sneer at sailors as the scum of the prisons, tosspots and ruffians, rogues and vagabonds. But they're brave and honest in their fashion if treated right.'

'Do you have to go out tonight, or have you asked friends in to eat with us?' asked Liza, still clutching a handful of his silken shirt as though she were afraid that if she let go her elusive husband might disappear once more.

Drake looked guilty. 'Well, love, I have asked a few fellows in for a bite. So many people want to hear about the voyage, and some of them sank money in the venture, so I feel they deserve a tale, if little more.'

'Good,' Liza said cheerfully. 'I had the cooks sweating over the preparation of a fine meal as soon as I knew that you would be free to come to me today. There is food out in the kitchens for fifty, I dare say.'

But though her voice was light, her

words hid a degree of disappointment. She realised that he would be made much of here in London, as he was in Plymouth, but she had hoped for *one* evening alone together before the callers came. But bowing to the inevitable, she went to speak to the cooks, before going to her room to change into a new gown.

The company who sat round the elegantly appointed dining table was a mixed one. She greeted Ralegh and Sir Francis Walsingham, who eyed one another thoughtfully over her head, and then went on to smile a welcome to other noblemen and their wives.

'Sidney and Greville are in the Netherlands, otherwise they would have been here, for it was only fate that stopped them sailing with us,' Drake said blandly to some of his guests. Looking round his parlour, he was proud of what he saw there. Men—and women, too—who knew him to be no man of ancient lineage like themselves, yet were honoured to sit at his table. He smiled at Liza and she, though chattering with animation to pretty Penelope Rich, seemed to sense his eyes on her and, switching her gaze from the vivacious little face before her, smiled back with a gaiety and comprehension that warmed her husband's heart.

After they had eaten—and eaten well, thought Sir Francis proudly—his guests called for an account of his voyage whilst they toyed with sweetmeats and fruit.

He agreed, knowing as he had said to his wife earlier that his guests would boast the next day of how they had heard the story from the hero's own lips.

So, in the hush of a summer evening, with the street noises outside muted by the thick old walls of the house and the smallness of the mullioned windows, Sir Francis Drake held his listeners spellbound with the story of the most audacious Spaniard-baiting that those present could have imagined, or dreamed of.

He told how their voyage had gone, from the capturing of a French salt barque closely followed by the taking of the cargo of 'poor john' from a Spanish vessel. The French ship, he explained, he had paid for in full already as he had vowed to do; he could not have been very flattered by the murmurs of astonishment this brought forth from his audience! He told of their first landing at Bayona, in Vigo Bay. Here, they had the double good fortune both to capture the Vigo Cathedral plate, and to release from imprisonment (and a certain death as heretics) some English sailors being held captive in the prisons of the town.

Drake glossed over the failure to capture the treasure fleet, but, instead, held his listeners enchanted with the romantic story of the attack on Santiago. Christopher Carleill and his soldiers had taken up their position overlooking the city, whilst Drake and the fleet waited offshore. Then, as Carleill began to stealthily advance, he realised it was already a ghost-town. The mere mention of Drake had been enough to send the inhabitants flying for the hills, but they had left fifty cannon, ready loaded.

'It was 17th November, and we knew back in England you would all be celebrating the accession of Queen Elizabeth to the throne twenty-seven years ago,' Drake said with a smile. 'So good old Chris decided to fire the cannon so that we, too, could join in the rejoicings. Fortunately, we at sea realised the great salute was not an attack, and we fired our cannon as well. So the Spanish, quite without meaning to, took part in the Accession Day celebrations of her Majesty, Queen of England.'

There was a general laugh and some cheers, and Liza realised how neatly Drake had got out of having to admit that once again he had been forced to leave without any loot other than the captured guns.

He did not gloss over the attack of fever which he thought they had caught whilst in the empty city of Santiago, but hurried over it, for he had no desire to recall the many who had died in one short week. But he told of the merrymaking at St Kitts, and of how the men had grown strong and fit again after cleaning the ships and planning the next venture.

For Drake and the other captains, in a council of war, had decided to attack Santo Domingo, the third city in the Spanish Empire.

'It was said to be unassailable, so strongly was it guarded,' he told his guests. 'Yet we did it—with the help of the Cimarrons who hold the mountains behind the town. They have no love for the Spanish, who would kill them off, if they could. So the Cimarrons dealt with the guards patrolling the beaches, for our fleet had been spotted, of course, and they were wary of a night attack. But the Cimarrons did their task

151

well, and on New Year's Day we landed a goodish force on the beach with Carleill here in charge, of course. They crept up to the foothills, to hide until the dawn attack.'

'When did the Governor suspect?' asked Walsingham, highly entertained to think of his son-in-law, the suave and self-confident young Christopher Carleill, condescending to crouch upon the earth in ambush.

'Luck was with us,' admitted Drake with a grin, which was shared by Carleill sitting further up the long board. 'The President has a pretty niece and she married a local fellow, so the Governor was not prepared for an attack. Probably still muzzy from the celebrations—you know these Spaniards! Anyway, the city was captured, our flag broken out and all evil Spaniards gone from within the walls (for the only good Spaniards are dead ones, and to our knowledge only one died that day) before midnight, so the city was ours on New Year's Day.'

Men and women chatted softly as Drake paused, collecting his thoughts. He told them of how his own negro boy had gone out to receive a message from a Spanish officer under a flag of truce and was brutally murdered, and how he had sworn that he would hang two friars each day, on the spot where the lad had died, until the guilty officer was executed. Having extracted his revenge, he then took a ransom for the life of the city itself, after a month's rest there. Twenty-five thousand ducats—not as much as he had hoped for—and the city was plaguey hard to burn, he told his listeners.

'Why burn it?' someone asked.

'Mere threats would only have made the Spaniards run faster,' Carleill explained for Drake. 'They had to see the buildings burn before they would part with a groat. But we burned the shipping in the harbour anyway, and only carried one ship with us—a Frenchy, by the cut of her. Then we collected our money and made for Cartagena.'

Having refreshed himself with a pull of wine, Drake took up the story again, telling of frightening defences at Cartagena—the foreshore sown with poisoned stakes, a chained entrance to the harbour, and citizens who had had three weeks' warning of their approach.

Then he told how, once again, past friendship with the natives had proved useful. It was they who warned Drake about the poisoned stakes and advised him that there were two royal galleys in the harbour, though they were not prepared for war.

'They should have been, had they listened to their own intelligence forces,' Carleill put in quietly. 'But I suppose they thought we would never get past the chained harbour mouth to seaward, and, if we had, the shore batteries in the fort would have shot our ships to matchwood. But even though they were badly organised, they fought well.'

'Yes, for Spaniards,' admitted Drake, and there was a general laugh as Carleill, with a wry grin, altered his comment to: 'Considering they were Spaniards, they fought bravely enough.'

'Plunder was—disappointing,' Drake said, casting a sideways look at Carleill which made that young gentleman grin again. 'However, I had the Bishop Tristan de Oribe practically weeping on to my feet when he came to talk of the ransom of the city.'

'Why? Did he want the city so badly?' asked Liza curiously.

'Badly enough, my pretty. But no, I had

been ransacking the Governor's personal papers and found a letter from that so-called King of Spain, in which he referred to me as "that corsair". I was in a fury, I can tell you. I told the Bishop I'd accept only an apology of the utmost sincerity before I'd even consider sparing the city. You should have seen that man grovel!'

'Why "so-called King"? Do you dispute his kingship?' asked Ralegh, amused.

'He's too small to be called a king, Ralegh. Too mean and petty. Shut away from his people, caring for nothing but the fruits of the Inquisition he has brought into being. And such a man, daring to refer to me as a corsair.'

'I—I don't see that's so terrible—' protested Liza, but could not continue her sentence. Drake gave a roar.

'Corsair? Pirate? *Me,* to be called such a thing? I am a Knight of the Realm, I sailed under the Royal Standard. Don't be a fool, Liza. He insulted me and the Queen by that word.'

Liza said no more and, seeing her suitably chastened, Drake patted her head kindly.

'Never mind. But if you want to enrage me, little Liza, you'll know what name to put your tongue to.'

Amidst the general laughter and talk which followed, Drake was pensive, planning how to end his story dramatically.

'We sailed from Cartagena more because of the unhealthy situation of the spot than anything else,' he said at last. 'From there, we went to San Agustin in Florida; the place you'll have heard of where the settlement of Huguenots were massacred. I wanted to attack it and burn it to the ground because, having got rid of the French, the Spaniards moved in, of course. We landed in the misty early morning. A small party, for stealth was important. We did not know, you see, where the Spaniards had set up the colony which took the place of the original San Agustin settlement of the Protestants. We were creeping carefully along the bank of a creek, with the beginnings of light turning the sky to gold, when we heard the last sound we expected. Over the screech of the awakening parakeets we heard the notes of a fife; someone was playing the Prince of Orange song. So strange it was, so portentous, that at first it seemed supernatural. Then we crept quietly through the undergrowth, for we knew that only a friend to the Protestant cause—and a brave one—would play such a tune in Spanish territory.

'We came on him at last. A slim, dark-haired young man clad in rags, sitting on a rock playing his defiant song on a home-made fife. He looked at us as though we were ghosts, but such welcome ones, for he had been in Spanish hands for six years and would have been glad even of honourable death to discharge him from a life of such misery. His name was Nicholas Borgoignon, and the tales he had to tell us! About the native Indians of the country, who in exchange for useful presents would allow one to search in the Appalachian mountains for gold, rubies and diamonds, and find them, too! He offered to guide us to the new San Agustin and we saw to his ills and gave him fresh clothes, and when the musicians on board the *Elizabeth Bonaventure* played for him the tears stood in his great brown eyes. A nice lad, Nicholas.'

He paused, seeing in his mind's eye the young man who had been through so much as he stepped ashore in France—the land he had never believed he would see again. Good had come from the voyage, apart from the good which came with any harm to Spain, in his mind.

'So? He took you to this place?'

The question brought Drake back to the present. The candlelit room, warm with the summer dusk and the press of people, rich with the smell of good food. How different from that strange, unfriendly, swampy coast!

'Yes, Nicholas led us to the fort. But though it was deserted, the Spaniards were only hiding out in the jungle to ambush us. However, we managed better than they had expected. We took the garrison's pay-chest—or at least its contents—and removed everything that might prove useful to the Spaniards. Then we razed the fort to the ground and got back into our pinnaces, leaving only one dead man behind—Anthony Powell. He acted bravely but foolishly and was shot by a Spaniard. But it would have been madness to imperil our lives and our ships by searching inland for treasure, however great. And I had promised Ralegh to see how his settlers in Virginia were making out, had I not, Walter? So we sailed for Charleston Harbour. They need provisions, but are doing their best to settle. Then we came home, leaving the Spanish King cursing and licking his wounds.'

The murmurs of talk swelled to a confused gabble of sound as the party saw Drake lean back comfortably in his chair and sink his teeth into an apple. They had heard the story, and could now talk it over amongst themselves; hear what the men who had been with Drake and sat at this table thought of the voyage.

For Liza's part, she knew the little details of the story, such as how Tom Moone met his death, and the manner in which they had avoided the poisoned stakes, would come out in snatches of conversation through the months ahead. Her mind recoiled, however, from how few months there might be before he was off once more, for already in the talk around her she heard constant references to 'next time'.

When they had speeded the last departing guests on their way with good wishes, and were wending their weary way upstairs, Drake said suddenly, 'I almost forgot! There is a gift for you which cannot wait till morning. Isabelle!'

From the back of the house came Isabelle, leading by one hand an Indian girl of quite amazing beauty. She had hair black as jet in two long plaits which reached to her knees, and even in the ill-fitting gown of a maidservant it was obvious that she had a body as beautiful as her face.

'I have my negro boy, chosen to replace the one who was killed. This girl is for you. We call her Rose, and perhaps if she and the boy mate she will bear children, and then their children can be servants for our children. Do you like her?'

Liza murmured, 'Does she speak English?'

The girl answered for herself. 'Yes, milady. The men on the ship teach me. I was a slave to the Spaniard. Now I come to be your servant.'

Liza turned rather helplessly to Isabelle, who was eyeing her protégée narrowly. 'I'm sure that Belle will see you are looked after, Rose,' she said as pleasantly as she could. 'I'll speak to you in the morning, when I'm not so tired. Good night.'

As they entered their bedchamber Drake said casually, 'She's a good girl, Rose. The Spaniards gave her some wretched papist name, so we christened her Rose, for she is a flower amongst her people for looks. I thought she might please you.'

The tentative note in his voice made Liza answer more sharply than she intended.

'Did she please you, then? On the long voyage home, did she lie on your bed with her hair flowing across your naked bodies, and gaze at you out of those swimming black eyes whilst you enjoyed her?'

Drake gasped, then swung out his hand and hit Liza across the face with such force that she lost her balance and fell on her knees, swaying with the violence of the blow.

'How dare you suggest I'd take advantage of a slave girl.'

His voice was low and controlled, but Liza saw that his hands shook. Without answering, she got unsteadily to her feet and went towards her dressing-room. Drake followed her and when she tried to shut the door in his face, prevented her with contemptuous ease.

'You're a spoilt, over-indulged child.' His voice was icy. 'So you thought a corsair was no bad thing to call your husband, eh? Why, the lowest sailor on my ship would tell you that I'm a man of principle. Did I ever try to make love to you before our marriage? Did I not wait until I could control my ardour? Why

161

then should you accuse me of changing the morals of a lifetime in order to play the fool with a slave girl?'

'Because she's beautiful, and you'd been without a woman for many months,' muttered Liza in a low voice. One side of her mouth was swelling where he'd hit her and she was afraid he would notice her shaking hands. 'If you didn't desire her, why did you bring her back here, to live under our roof as a servant? Why not let one of the other men take her, for I'm sure the whole fleet don't share your wonderful principles.'

'Isabelle is married now, and may become pregnant and leave you. Rose is a clever creature and has been trained as a lady's maid. If you hadn't behaved like a spoilt child throwing bad words in a fit of temper, I would have said that since you'd taken a dislike to the girl, she could go elsewhere. As it is, you'll have to grow used to her. And don't think you can ill-treat her with impunity, because her English is reasonably good and my Spanish, as you know, is excellent. Soon enough, I'd hear of it, and you'd find out how severe my displeasure can really be.'

'I wouldn't ill-treat her,' said Liza

indignantly. 'Why should I? Even if she were your mistress I couldn't hurt her. She's alone in a strange land.'

'I need no mistress,' Drake said wearily. 'Sometimes it seems a wife is more of a trial than a comfort.'

He turned from the doorway, and began to remove his clothes listlessly.

Liza felt the tears trickle down her cheeks. She had meant to be so good, so loving! Their first night together after the long absence, and they were quarrelling! She ran to him, her gown and farthingale cast aside, comical in a chemise and stockings, with her hair still piled Court-fashion and her jewellery in place.

He tried to repulse her, but the words, 'I'm sorry, I'm so sorry, my darling,' and the hot tears that fell on his hands turned his annoyance from her to himself.

'I was harsh, needlessly so. You spoke through ignorance of my discipline aboard ship. Why, love, I couldn't lower my moral standards and then expect anything better of my men, could I? Now stop crying, it's all forgotten. If you want Rose to go, she shall. Come to bed, little one, and let me make you forget our quarrel.'

'Rose can stay. I'm sure I'll like her

when we get to know one another,' said Liza between sniffs.

Between the sheets they made up their differences in the best way of all. But when her husband slept, Liza lay thoughtfully awake. Fortunately, she had not said so in the heat of the quarrel, but she wondered now just how 'normal' was it to be able to hold back your natural desires with a girl as lovely as Rose sleeping on a straw pallet in your cabin. 'I kept her by me, to save others from temptation,' he had told her piously. He had not needed to assure her further that he had never enjoyed Rose. No man in his senses would admit to having slept in the same room as a young and beautiful woman unless he really was innocent of seduction. Yet, stupidly, her very certainty made her uneasy. Why had he not taken her until she had seduced him with pretended slumber? Why had he asked a large party home, the very first time he'd seen his wife for ten months? She had half-expected him to come into her room when she was changing, and indeed he had done so. But though his eyes had dwelt appreciatively upon the curve of breast and buttock, he had not been tempted to tumble her—and she his lawful wife! She had been ashamed, then, of her own feelings. The very *smell* of his remembered masculinity had sent surges of desire through her, so that she had come very near to offering herself. Only pride had prevented her from doing so.

Yet he was not in any way effeminate; he had just made love to her with a force and vigour greater than she had known before. Perhaps, she thought helplessly, he had been forced to control his emotions too much, so that he found it more difficult to release them than other men.

Sighing, she allowed herself to be overcome by sleep; to drift into a world where she walked over sunlit grass with her hand clasped in Frank's, where they found a little dell in a wood—and where he made love to her with all the gentleness she had known, and all the passion that her body told her she could have known.

★ ★ ★ ★

Rose fitted into the Drake household without difficulty, partly because she was sensible and quick to learn, and partly because Isabelle had taken a fancy to the intelligent, good-natured Indian girl.

Liza, too, in spite of her initial prejudice, soon learned to love Rose. The girl had been so badly treated by her Spanish owners that she considered London a paradise and would have died for Liza or Drake. As to her morals, it was soon obvious that in this respect at least Drake had been keeping his men safe from Rose rather than vice versa, when he kept her close! To please was her one desire, and she had pleased almost every male member of the household before they set off to Plymouth once more. Except Drake, that is. He tried lecturing her, he tried keeping a constant watch on her by setting Jack, the negro, to spy on her every movement. Everything proved useless. Rose was a delightful little creature, with the manners of a saint and the morals of an alleycat, as Isabelle put it.

'She's very fond of you, though, Belle,' Liza remarked as they packed her grand London gowns. 'And she'll do anything for a friend. You'll have to watch that she doesn't show you how much she likes you by offering herself to Mark!'

'If that hussy casts her slanting, wanton

eyes in Mark's direction ...' began Isabelle, then grinned sheepishly. 'Well, I'll just have to keep Mark busy myself and hope he doesn't find Rose beautiful.'

'All men must find her beautiful, for she is,' Liza said calmly. 'Do you know how old she is?'

'Eighteen? Nineteen?'

'So far as we can make out, she's twelve going on thirteen,' Liza told her, laughing. 'These foreign girls mature early, don't they, Belle?'

'Lord!' said Belle promptly. 'Knows every trick in the book at that age. She'll be a whore at fifteen and dead at twenty.'

'Sir Francis says she needs a firm hand and a good example to make her see the error of her ways,' Liza told Isabelle. 'Sometimes I think he's right about the firm hand—she needs beating!'

'Sir Francis will marry her to Jack as soon as she's old enough and perhaps that will keep her out of mischief,' said Isabelle consolingly.

'Oh, yes. Make an adultress of the girl, is that what you mean? About the only man she hasn't slept with is Jack—she says he's ugly and black.'

Laughing, the two girls shut the last trunk and called for rope to tie it safely. Tomorrow they would be on their way home, to Plymouth.

8

TO ANNOY THE DON

Drake was home this time for eight months, before setting off on a major voyage once more. Liza, preparing his gear for him, knew that as usual his main worry was only that the Queen might change her mind, or take from him some of his power to hurt the Spaniards.

'He sailed to the Netherlands and parleyed, and brought the Earl of Leicester home for the trial of Mary Queen of Scots, but he says it wasn't like being at sea; it was more like running messages,' Liza told Belle as she folded clean shirts into a pile and sprinkled lavender between each garment.

'If Mary hadn't been executed, perhaps they wouldn't be going to sea against Philip,' argued Belle reasonably. 'And if Leicester hadn't been on hand to jog the Queen's elbow, who knows when she would have signed the death warrant—if ever?'

'There is change all around,' sighed Liza. She was thinking of the death of Sir Philip Sidney, killed in battle the year before. And even that thought brought a worse one in its train. Sidney had only been badly wounded—it had taken him three long and terrible weeks to die.

'Why do you suppose the Queen takes Philip's threat to invade England seriously enough to send the fleet into Spanish waters?' asked Belle.

'Because whatever Philip may have threatened and protested, he couldn't have had much faith in Mary Stuart. But now that she's dead, he can take the crown for himself in an almost legal way. He *was* married to Queen Mary, and James of Scotland is far off. So, thank God, she's decided to take the advice of her ministers and do Spain what harm she can instead of waiting until they attack us.'

'I wonder how Mark will get on? It's his first sea voyage,' said Belle restlessly. 'Suppose—oh, well, milady, you have to suppose as well, so you understand me.'

'Indeed I do, Belle. But I truly believe Mark is doing the right thing,' Liza assured the other girl. 'Times are hard for the man who owns no land—though Mark is a skilled tradesman, he can earn only fourpence a day—we would be fined if we overpaid him, and he would be fined also! You are married, yet you are afraid to have a child because you need your earnings as well as those of your husband. Well, if this voyage is fairly successful Mark may be able to buy the land you've got your eye on, and build a nice little house upon it. Folk with a small farm *and* a trade do very well; it's landless men who have to struggle to feed their families who resort to begging, or stealing—or die, starving.'

'Yes, and I'd like my children to have schooling,' Belle said wistfully. 'Here's me, past twenty, and I can barely read and write. Mark is worse, for he can do neither. Yet Rose, the little monkey, can read and write Spanish and is beginning to do both in English, too. My children shall have their chance; Mark is as determined as I am.'

'Trust in Sir Francis and the English ships,' Liza told her. 'I know this voyage is supposed to be only a punitive expedition to stop the Spaniards sailing against us in war, but I'll be bound that a little booty will cling to the English ships and thus to the sailors' pockets, whatever their high and noble intentions.'

With a lighter heart, Belle continued to stack her master's garments in the wooden crates.

★ ★ ★ ★

'Don't cry, Belle, they've been gone for over a week now. Come, let us walk on the Hoe in the cool of the evening and look at the sea. I often find it calms me to know Sir Francis sails that same sea and, in a way, is almost with me.'

The two women walked down to the Hoe, quickening their pace as they saw a crowd had gathered. In their midst was a messenger on a tall horse. Both were travel-stained and weary, and the messenger looked angry.

He saw Liza and hailed her with relief.

'My Lady—I come with a message for your husband. These good people tell me that the fleet has sailed—indeed, I can see it has. But my orders are that if the bird has flown (beg pardon, my Lady) I was to organise a ship to follow with the letters. However, none of these fellows knows of a vessel—or so they say.'

'Most of the shipping has gone with the fleet,' put in Belle helpfully. 'Of course, there may be a fishing barque or two, but they are maybe afraid of being snapped up by a Spaniard—or cursed by a Drake.'

There was a general laugh.

'The message would hinder the enterprise,' a small, walnut-skinned man standing by Liza said quietly. 'But it won't reach your Ladyship's husband, not by the hands of a Plymouth man.'

Liza was quiet for a moment, then caught the eye of another man in the crowd. It was a bright blue eye, familiar in some way.

'Who's that?' Liza murmured to Belle.

'One of John Hawkins' bastards. Plymouth is full of 'em,' Belle said succinctly. 'He's only just got back from a voyage, or he'd have gone with our men.'

'Young man.' Liza's voice was quiet and yet authoritative. 'Could you sail after the fleet?' Their eyes met, and after the shortest of hesitations the man replied, 'Yes, if you say so, Lady Liza.'

'And is there a suitable boat?'

'There's a pinnace, Lady Liza. It belongs

173

to Captain Wynter, but I'm sure he'd lend it in such a cause.'

'Good. Get a crew and sail when it is safe to do so.'

Once again, the blue eyes and the brown met, full of meaning.

'Certainly, my Lady.'

He turned and was gone, hurrying down the Hoe towards the harbour. Liza turned to the messenger.

'You're tired,' she said gently. 'Come to my house, and I'll see the servants find you a clean bed and a decent supper. Your horse will be well looked after in the stables. Are you satisfied now that your task is done?'

He glanced down at her. Shrewd, tired eyes, worldly and kind. 'Yes, indeed I am, Lady Elizabeth. I would not want it any other way for the world, for I am a true Englishman. I know your house. If you'll forgive me I'll make my way there at once, before I fall asleep in the saddle.'

'So *that's* all right,' Liza said to Belle as they walked homeward. 'No son of Hawkins, whether born the right or wrong side of the blanket, would betray my husband. We'll not see the fleet in Plymouth until its task has been accomplished.'

★ ★ ★ ★

The pinnace, as Liza had anticipated, never caught up with the fleet. Instead, it sailed back into Plymouth Sound, telling of fierce gales which had forced the vessel to abandon its search. The fact that the crew brought back with them a prize they had taken was glossed over with a quick shrug. The fortunes of war are strange!

★ ★ ★ ★

'Away for not even twelve weeks, and he brings back a king's ransom—or a queen's,' Liza said exultantly to Belle, as she busied herself in her room at Buckland, preparing for her husband's return from London. 'And from the little he was able to tell me before he left for the Court, he has destroyed so much Spanish shipping—and so much Spanish self-confidence—that there will be no war this year. As to next—' She shrugged. 'Perhaps they'll sail again. Who knows?'

'Now we shall buy the land, and Mark

175

can begin to build our home,' said Belle contentedly. 'The only trouble is, milady, Mark *enjoyed* being absent from home. Well, he says he enjoyed the adventure, but that's what he really meant. He swears he will always accompany Sir Francis in future, even on a voyage round the world, if your husband should again wish to undertake such a mission.'

Liza laughed at the mixture of pleasure and horror in Isabelle's voice.

'We mustn't complain, Belle. Your husband has tasted the freedom of the ocean, and the companionship which comes with adventure. But whilst they are together, so are we! You will have to learn patience as I have done. Anyway, at least your husband can disembark from his ship and come straight to your side. Mine, alas, has to speak with the Queen, the Council, other Admirals. That's why he posted off up to London after only one short night in my company.'

She smiled reminiscently at the thought of his return. The enfolding hug, whilst he stuttered out how the Spanish shipping had burned, how the towns had burned, and how he had seized the *San Felipe* with the richest cargo imaginable, to make the voyage a financial as well as a strategic success.

'I thought he posted off up to London in a rage, to see William Borough hanged as a traitor,' Belle said with a grin.

'Oh, as to that ...' Liza protested airily. Then, her curiosity getting the better of her, 'Sir Francis did not speak of it to me. What exactly did Borough do to bring down my husband's wrath upon his head, Belle?'

'Well, from what Mark has told me, it was Borough who caused the first spark between them. He's a naval man, used to doing things the traditional way. Sir Francis, on the other hand, does not go into a battle with a preconceived plan. He waits until he gets to the scene of the clash, sums up the defences, seeks out the enemy's weakest point and then begins to formulate his attack.'

'Isn't that how it should be done?' asked Liza, rather indignantly.

Isabelle shrugged. 'Probably. Mark thinks so, at any rate. But the point which annoyed Borough was that Sir Francis did not call all his captains and commanders to meet, discuss, vote on each move, etc. He merely outlined his moves, and told his captains to follow the *Elizabeth Bonaventure*. Mark say he thinks Borough might not have complained if his advice had been sought, and then not followed. But the fellow could not abide to be ignored altogether.'

'But, surely, if Sir Francis was proved right by subsequent events, what possible cause for complaint did Borough have?' asked Liza rather doubtfully.

'Well, although Borough was horrified by the un-naval way Sir Francis behaved in Cadiz harbour, such a resounding victory spoke for itself. He said nothing then, save modified grumbles. But when Drake proposed to seize the Cape by a surprise attack on Sagres Castle (another invincible Spanish fortification, my Lady) then Borough could contain himself no longer. He wrote a letter to Sir Francis which put your husband in a great rage. He took Borough's command away from him, and gave it to Captain Marchant. Borough he put under arrest.'

'Good Lord, that seems a bit severe,' protested Liza.

'Well, Mark thinks he was a bit overwhelmed by the worries and quick actions he had to take. He got it into his head that Borough might be another Doughty and question his authority. But at least he did not try to act for himself this time. Doughty is dead because he had to be. But Borough will put his case before the Queen and Council, no doubt.'

'Oh, well,' said Liza. 'Borough will get his just deserts, I'm sure.'

Belle was silent. She had heard more from Mark than she had felt it wise to repeat. That Drake had accused Borough of mutiny and sentenced him to death, after he had re-taken command of his ship, the *Lion*, from John Marchant and sailed away to England in her. And though most of the sailors and officers were on Drake's side, there were others who said that Borough had a right to his opinion, after all. He was a naval commander of repute, and second-in-command. Yet the slight courtesy of allowing him to voice his thoughts had not been given to him.

And although the courage and daring Sir Francis had shown in his attack on Cadiz could only be admired, and actually taking the Cape of St Vincent and holding it whilst at the same time destroying any shipping that sailed in and out of Lisbon made even Belle's half-comprehending mind fill with awe, she could not help feeling terror also.

Mark sailed with Drake. Mark was her beloved, the reason for her existence. Yet he assured her that nothing he expected of his men was beneath Drake. When they burned the gates of Sagres Castle because they had no cannon or siege train, Drake laboured like a navvy with timber and pitch, firing it with his own hand, his muscles aching as theirs did.

'You're silent, Belle. What are you thinking?'

'Oh, only that my husband left me with all his love, and has come back tied to Sir Francis' apron strings, milady. By the way, Rose is standing by the door, waiting for the master to ride into view. She'll call us, so we can be downstairs to greet him.'

'Well, if you'll fix a pink rosebud in my hair we might as well go down now, for I'm as ready as I ever shall be,' said Liza, surveying herself critically in the mirror. She and Belle were half-way down the stairs when they heard Rose's chirruping cry.

'Milady, milady, the master is riding up the drive!'

Belle watched indulgently as Liza took

the rest of the stairs at a run, and saw Sir Francis enter the hall and fling his arms round his pretty wife. Then she turned and went back to Liza's bedchamber. There was work for her to complete before she could rejoin her own husband.

★ ★ ★ ★

'God knows what is *wrong* with England!' cried Drake suddenly.

They were in their bedchamber getting ready for bed. Drake was already stripped to his shirt, Liza to her petticoats. All evening she had been aware that there was something bothering her husband. But she knew him well enough by now to know that whatever it was, he would tell her in his own way and his own time. So now she sat down beside him on the bed and turned up her eyes to his face.

He put his arm round her and squeezed her shoulders gently.

'Poor Liza, to be married to me. I went to London thinking—no, not thinking, *knowing*—that I had done well. That my Queen and country would be proud of me. But what do I hear at Court? "That fellow Drake, making trouble for us again.

Just because they made him a Knight, you know, he thinks he can do what he will. The Queen swears he exceeded his instructions and she wants to know nothing of what went on at Cadiz, or Cape St Vincent, or Lisbon." '

The grip round Liza's shoulders tightened, and Drake's voice went dully on.

'What of the Spanish shipping that was being got ready to sail against England? They can afford to ignore it now, for it will certainly not sail this year. What of the garrisons burned or razed to the ground, the fleet fishing for supplies on the codbanks—every one of them destroyed and their catch with them? Ah-ha, the Queen was gracious enough to accept my gifts from the *San Felipe*—the King of Spain's own particular treasure ship, more heavily laden than all the rest. But as to the foolish buccaneer who risked his life and those of his men a dozen times for her sake—him she will not acknowledge.'

'Oh, my darling, they can't treat you like this,' Liza cried, gripping her fists so tightly that her nails dug into the flesh. 'You did not exceed one jot of your duty—she surely does not hope for *peace* with Spain?'

'Spain has no choice for now but peace,'

Drake told her. 'But the future, does she never think of the future? She is a brilliant woman with a man's brain, so she cannot believe that we have won. We have brought a much-needed respite, that's all. I sent from Cape St Vincent for more ships and soldiers, so that we could hold the Cape indefinitely. But once she realised we were safe for this year, it was like asking for the moon. I took her papers—papers saying how King Philip would enter England in force, and put to death by sword or fire all persons over seven years of age. The Queen herself—our Queen, Liza—was to be burnt at the stake in front of St Paul's Cathedral as a lesson to the populace.'

Liza heard the breath catch in his throat and knew that he wept. Without shame, the man who had stood before the castle gates at Sagres with the cannon shots whistling round his ears sat beside her, crying. And she knew it was not for himself he cried. He cried for England, and that strange, straight-backed woman, Elizabeth Tudor.

★ ★ ★ ★

So though he was allowed, somewhat

grudgingly, to keep a small fleet anchored in Plymouth Sound—though more ships swung at anchor in Gillingham Reach—the summer was an anxious one for Drake. He pestered everyone—the Queen, Burghley, Leicester—to let him sail once more, and put a stop to the invasion force, this time for good. But his pleas were ignored.

So one warm day at the height of summer, Liza persuaded her husband to go with her to the outskirts of the Buckland estate where Mark and Isabelle were building their farmhouse. The work was in progress with Mark very much the master, and they were welcomed cheerfully, and introduced into the art of building a modern, well-constructed dwelling.

'These timbers are oak, of course,' Mark said instructively, laying his hand on a stout post of pale, well-polished wood. 'We are not yet rich and, anyway, I've no great love for bricks and tile. So these thin laths will be nailed between the posts and beams, and filled up with plaster, layer on layer, until it's sturdy and strong, yet smooth and beautiful.'

'Wattle and daub, in effect. Very sensible,' Sir Francis said, nodding. 'Our house in Plymouth is the same, though it is tiled. What will be your roofing, then? Thatch?'

'Yes, and reed thatch, too. More expensive, of course, but it will last out *our* lifetime,' said Mark contentedly. He gave a friendly wave of his hand that was yet half a salute, and turned back to supervising the men who were laying the floorboards carefully in place.

Liza and Sir Francis stood back and watched. Already the house was beginning to take shape. A neat, well-built place it looked, too, with its shape outlined in posts and cross beams so that one could see the big parlour, the study where Mark would work out the yield of his acres, the airy kitchen and stillroom, with the planned areas for the dairy and outbuildings, which would be built later. Upstairs, the principal bedroom jutted over the large windows of the parlour, and two smaller bedrooms could be reached through it, and above yet again were two little attic rooms.

'It will be a beautiful house,' Liza said enthusiastically as they stood watching, the sun hot on their shoulders. 'Mark is a fine carpenter and will work so lovingly on the carving that Belle says her panelling will be the finest in the country. Already he is studying diligently how to grow the best and most sensible crops on his land, and where he should have his permanent pasture for his beasts.'

'Sometimes I think it would be best if I had never wanted to better my lot in the world but had been content, like Mark, to follow others,' growled Drake, and looked sideways at Liza. 'He doesn't worry about the possibilities of war with Spain because he has faith in me and the Queen to stop it or win it—he doesn't mind which. He builds with pleasure for his children, never seeing the things that may come with the Spaniards if they conquer our island—the Inquisition, the slaughter, the subjection of all people, great and small.'

'But surely such a thing can't happen?' Liza said incredulously. 'You've stopped it for this year and King Philip may be tired of this never-ending talk of the conquest of England.'

They turned to mount their horses and ride home to Buckland.

'I saw preparations at Lisbon and other places which made me certain that war will come some day, when the Spaniards think we are unprepared,' Drake told her uneasily. 'Their plan is plain enough—a

186

mighty flotilla of vessels carrying huge numbers of troops. And invasion barges coming from Parma, across the Narrow Seas, to reinforce their numbers. It would be easy enough for them to burn the towns near the coast and massacre the people, if they are allowed to land. Our men are brave, but we could not hope to bring a trained army against the invaders. Yet the Queen can laugh, and call me a warrior who wishes to fight for the joy of it!'

'Have you told her this, Frank?'

'I tried, Liza; I tried. But she will no longer listen to my advice. She says she will hear her peacemakers for a change. Believe me, my love, there is nothing worse for a man of action than inaction, disbelief, scorn and derision when he can see danger threatening all he holds most dear.'

He paused, and his frown darkened. 'If she had seen the things I've seen,' he said quietly, with a controlled violence somehow more frightening than raving. 'I've seen men worn to the bone and covered in sores from long imprisonment, blinded by light after months of total darkness, robed in yellow to show their Protestant faith, being carted from the torture chambers of the Inquisition to the agony of the fire so that Philip can warm his shrivelled soul at the flame of their martyrdom.'

'Yet she sees so clearly most things that happen,' Liza said timidly.

'Sees, yes. But one of her favourite remarks is, "I see, but I do nothing." Well, if she does nothing this time, it may be the end of us all, Liza. The end of England.'

* * * *

Yet by the time winter came, the Queen was beginning to listen to Drake again, and to take heed of his advice. A big fleet lay ready in Sutton Pool, others were being prepared under the Lord Admiral Howard, and Plymouth streets were a-jostle with sailors, merchants and pretty girls.

'If only she would let us attack the Spanish fleet *before* it sails,' groaned Drake, pacing the quay and gazing out over the sea as though if he stared hard enough he could conquer even the curve of the earth. 'Our spies have told us plain enough—the plan is that the fleet shall bring a great army and meet up with Parma in the Low Countries. Then we should have to fight against the odds indeed, if it came to a land battle.'

'Can't you harass the shipping so that they never land?' Liza asked fearfully, thinking of the narrow streets of Plymouth and her friends who lived so near their beloved sea.

'So much depends on the wind,' Drake explained patiently. 'Suppose a sudden gale should blow up and pen us into the harbour? Such a gale could even aid the Spanish ships to attack our shores whilst the might of England's seamen were powerless—landlocked by the very wind which would be our friend afloat.'

Liza glanced at her husband's face. It seemed, suddenly, to be the very embodiment of all things English. His mouth was tight with determination, but his eyes shone with a clear conviction. He would struggle, and he would fight—and so would all England. He would argue and complain—and so would all England. He would conquer—and so would all England.

Just at that moment, Liza knew with all the certainty in her being, that she was married to a great man and that other great men would work with him to keep their country safe. Then Drake moved, and the spell was broken.

'What shall we do?' she asked helplessly.

'We'll wait, sweetheart. Indeed, it's a task you are better fitted for than I, for wives such as you spend many weary weeks waiting. As for myself, it is only in the heat of action that I find fulfilment.'

By the time the apple blossom crowded the branches, sending its sweet, innocent perfume on every passing breeze, the Queen had agreed with Drake that the entire fleet should assemble off Plymouth and would sail as soon as the Armada vessels came into view. Liza watched, tears of pride running unheeded down her cheeks, as the puff-breasted sailing ships took up their positions. Her husband was Vice-Admiral of this whole perilous venture—and he a self-made man!

Yet still there were weeks of rumour and counter-rumour, command and counter-command, before the ships were to see the action they craved.

'I've never waved farewell and hello so often,' Liza complained crossly to Drake after the fleet's abortive attempt to attack the Spanish ships before they reached English waters.

'But it was the wind,' Drake told her with a smile, and she knew there could be no answer to *that.* Everyone's nerves were stretched to their utmost limit. In the taverns, men fought over a word, snarling like dogs because the very air they breathed was tension.

Yet there was no despair, no panic. Troops were marshalled and manoeuvres were practised so that everyone knew exactly their own position and responsibilities in the emergency that threatened.

'The very children play at soldiers, and plan an ambush,' Liza told Isabelle, who smiled gently and stroked her stomach. She was with child, and had quickened. National emergency or not, nothing could take the softness from her eyes and the gentle thickening of waist and once-flat belly.

Nothing? thought Liza, and dispelled the thought with a superstitious shudder. Something must happen soon or nerves would snap, and then God help them all.

As though it had been a signal, something did happen. The first sighting came from a Cornish fisherman fetching a cargo of salt from France. He had sailed, alone in his boat beneath the blue June sky, from the small port of Mousehole in Cornwall.

Looking idly about the empty ocean, he suddenly saw on the skyline some big ships. Remembering (if he had ever really forgotten) the Spaniards and their invasion fleet, he decided to investigate.

'I sailed that quiet and close, lads, I was almost under their bows before they saw me,' he told his at first somewhat sceptical drinking companions. 'I could see their billowing white sails with huge red crosses, and men were everywhere. Then they spotted me and one sailed in pursuit.' He laughed scornfully. 'Great, pot-bellied thing with its scarlet cross straining to catch at the breeze. I outsailed her quickly enough, and came straight to Plymouth, to tell our Drake. I'm not saying it was the whole of their precious Armada—damned sure it wasn't—but it was half a dozen mighty big vessels.'

The next man to come sailing home to England with news was Simons of Exeter, who was in command of a pinnace which had been sent to watch for the approach of the enemy. He had been chased by galleons with scarlet crosses on their sails, and three of his men had been injured by the enemy's fire.

Excitement in the whole country was high, but in Plymouth it rose to an almost unbearable pitch. Liza was on constant vigil, seeing that Drake had what rest he could, yet she could not stop him continually chafing against the decision to wait in Plymouth Sound and attack from there. Then the wind blew from the right direction and Drake came near to defying everyone and leaving the Sound.

Yet only a week later, on Friday, 19th July, Thomas Fleming, who had been watching from the Hoe, burst in upon Drake who was discussing strategy with other commanders in the small back garden of his town house.

'The Armada is in view, sailing down upon us from the Lizard,' Fleming shouted, his cheeks scarlet with exertion and excitement. 'I must go and get my crew on board,' and before he could be further questioned he had turned and dashed out of the garden and into the street beyond. They heard his quick feet running down towards the harbour, shouting out the news at the top of his stentorian voice.

'I'll get your things,' Liza said urgently.

'Will you send messages to the other captains? Captain Fleming surely cannot tell everyone?'

'No hurry. Remember the tide is on the flow and it will be several hours before we can begin to get the ships out of Plymouth Sound.' He licked his finger, laughing, and held it up to test the breeze. 'No wind to help us, either, darling. We must warp the ships out of their places as soon as we can, but that won't be yet.'

The other men had already scattered, to go to their houses to kiss their wives goodbye, or straight to their ships, to alert their men.

Liza, elated by the happy, confident ring in her husband's voice, stood on tiptoe to kiss him.

'I love you so, my master mariner,' she whispered. Then, aloud, 'Now I'd better see to my own packing, though most of my boxes are ready.'

She bustled into the house, calling for Isabelle. She had promised Sir Francis months ago that she and her household would pack up, and be constantly ready to move on his command to any place he should name. Thus, he had explained, she would be with him when he came, victorious, ashore.

She knew he never thought of defeat, because he dared not. He, of all men, knew the Spaniard. He knew why they no longer worked the richest mines in the world which their conquistadors had taken and held by the sword. Brutally, senselessly, they murdered the natives who had worked the mines. One could not expect a mighty Spaniard to stoop to manual labour. So there must be continual conquest if Spain was to remain rich and unmolested, having to rely upon those mines where the natives were still alive to garner the riches from the depths of the earth, or those places where slaves toiled with insufficient skill until they died of overwork and underfeeding.

This, he told her bitterly, was what the Spanish called 'colonising a country'. But though he never spoke of defeat, the urge to have his young wife prepared for every contingency was strong in him. So she and Isabelle would saddle their horses as soon as a message came, and follow Drake's commands to the letter.

The following day, Liza and Belle stood at the top of the Hoe and watched with awe and fear the might of Spain cruising in a great, crescent-shaped formation off the coast of Plymouth. Behind them, like dogs worrying cattle, sailed the English fleet. Even as the two girls watched, they saw the remnants of the Lord Admiral Howard's fleet, which had been unable to leave the day before because of victualling problems, sailing steadily out of Plymouth Sound.

On the Hoe the all-important beacon burned, its flames damped with wet turf so that it sent a great column of grey smoke curling into the air. A warning to watchers further along the coast that the Spanish Armada was at last within sight of the keepers of England.

9

BATTLE ON THE NARROW SEAS

On board the *Revenge,* discipline and hardihood alike did not need to be mentioned. All the crew were hand-picked, sailors of experience and discernment. They would obey their leader without question, knowing that he would not lead them to defeat.

Mark, looking at his fellow mariners, greeting those he had not seen for a few weeks, realised that never had morale on board a ship been higher. There was excitement, certainly. But it showed only in the taut muscles and eager eyes straining after the great Spanish fleet. There was none of the usual talking and boasting, dancing jigs and indulging in dreams of riches. They were here, every man-jack of them, for the sake of their country. They were ready to lay down their lives if need be so that England could remain the green island they loved. A place where they and their sweethearts could walk the quiet places unmolested, free to worship God in the way they chose, free to love, free to live clean and decent lives without fear crippling their minds as the Inquisition would cripple their bodies. Now that they had seen with their own eyes the undoubted strength of the Spanish empire, and the size and splendour of her ships, they knew that only with the giving of their last ounce of effort could the task of keeping the enemy from their shores be achieved.

Presently, a sharp-eyed lad in the crow's nest shouted that the Royal Standard had been hoisted at the fore in the *San Martin,* the flagship of the Spanish Armada of the Fleet, Medina-Sidonia. And everyone on the deck of the *Revenge* saw the slow swinging in towards the shore of the great, ponderous ships. Immediately, orders were given, cannons made ready, sailors became gunners. Within twenty minutes, the first battle was joined.

Mark, even in the incredible noise, heat and haze of ships at war, had to admire the sheer skill with which their craft was sailed. They would bear down upon a chosen galleon, swing level with her, deliver a broadside that raked her from stem to stern, and be turning again whilst the Spaniards were still trying in vain to get their heavy cannon into line with the small, swift ships.

At close quarters, one could see how huge were the galleons of Spain. Mark noticed with a quick stab of anxiety that every deck seemed to be packed with soldiery—a formidable invasion fleet, sure enough. But with the arrival of the ships which had left Plymouth late, they saw the signal for the ceasing of hostilities go up on the *Ark Royal.*

Wiping the sweat from his brow (for the heat on the lower gundeck was intense and the guns heavy), Mark joined in the ragged cheer which went up. For looking round, he and the rest of the crew realised why Lord Howard had decided to save their precious ammunition. Plymouth Sound had been passed. A fair wind blew at their backs. The Armada could not now threaten Plymouth.

With the closing of the gunports, Mark became once more body servant to Sir Francis and, as soon as he was clean and changed, went to wait upon his master in the oak-panelled cabin. Drake was entertaining a most distinguished visitor—Nicholas Ouseley, one of Walsingham's best spies against the Spaniard.

I'd sooner face the whole Armada, alone in a fisherman's barque, then have his job, Mark thought with a shiver, as he poured wine for the two men and listened to their talk.

'They are strong. God send they have as little seamanship as we expect,' remarked Ouseley.

'God send they have as little ammunition as we have,' remarked Drake grimly, then added with a grin, 'But they attack without cause, whilst we defend. That in itself should make us the stronger. The lioness which defends her cubs can win a battle against a male lion of twice her strength, they say. If I were a betting man (which I am not), I'd back the man who fights to protect his tiny child with his bare fists, against a paid bully with a knife.'

'They could never see it that way,' Nicholas Ouseley reminded him gently. 'They see themselves as crusaders, Knights Templar if you like, fighting to restore the true religion. You fight for a child, they for a place in heaven and angels' wings brush them to frenzy.'

'Faugh! I've seen their "true religion" at work, as you have. Many of them are as frightened of the Inquisition as a devout Protestant. Why, we have good Catholics in our fleet that I'd trust with my life—and so would the Queen, God bless her. But *Spaniards!* They *fear* their God, and must think Him without compassion if they believe He could love them for the devilish work they do in His name.'

'Well, whatever the reason for it, they fought back,' reminded Ouseley.

'True enough. It looks as though it may come to a good fight—and a sea fight at that, for we're not such fools as to try boarding ships brimming with soldiers and many times our size. So we must beware of close fighting. We must nip in, deal our punishment and nip out of range. No standing alongside in the swell, exchanging shot for shot. Precious little chance of a win if we fought the way they'd like us to. But if we're fed, and supplied with power and shot, we've nought to fear.'

'The Queen must see the necessity, Sir Francis. Surely she'll victual the fleet?'

Drake shrugged his broad shoulders. 'She's a proud and courageous woman. But we all know only too well, she fights to restore some sort of balance in the Treasury which was despoiled of its riches before she came to the throne. So she has to be careful with every groat. Sometimes too careful. And again, she's never trodden the decks of a ship slippery with blood and guts. Some of her advisers are the same, men though they may be. Walsingham is a man who understands, and so does Leicester, though his Dudley blood makes him spend needlessly. Burghley? I can't fathom the man. But then, that makes two of us, for he doesn't understand me, either.' He broke off and turned to Mark.

'Fetch me paper, ink and sand, lad. I've got despatches to write.'

Then, in the afternoon, Mark and his fellow sailors crowded to the ship's side to see one of the big galleons explode without an Englishman lifting a hand against her. The *San Salvadore* seemed to lift from the water with the force of the blast, and though flames began to lick along her paintwork, the Spaniards managed to control the fire. Even so, the big vessel was badly damaged; more of a liability now than an asset. She began to fall behind, and signals were busy aboard the Spanish ships, so that soon other vessels dropped back as well, to protect the crippled one from any quick and crafty English vessel that might take advantage of her plight when darkness fell.

Later still, the *Nuestra Señora del Rosario* got herself into trouble, and had to be escorted by two more Spanish galleons and a pinnace. Mark had not been on deck at the time, but his friend Jamie told him the Spanish ships seemed to him to have crossed each other accidentally, and the *Rosario* had had her foremast broken off level with the deck, where it had crashed across her mainyard. She was obviously not answering to her rudder, as she was being towed by a galleasse.

When darkness began to steal across the sky, the Admiral of the Fleet called a council of war. Mark went with his master, pulling his oar in the ship's galley which carried them from the *Revenge* to the *Ark Royal*. When Drake returned, he told his servant that they thought the Spanish might be attempting to attack the Isle of Wight, for if they could seize the island, what a base it would be for every sort of interference and invasion!

'We are to keep watch for the fleet

tonight, Mark,' said Sir Francis as they entered the cabin again, blinking in the glow from the lamps, comforting when compared with the chilly wind that was beginning to whistle around the deck. 'Call an officer to see that the big lantern is set on the poop, where the rest of the fleet can see it.'

'Yes, sir. Will you be getting a sleep now, sir?'

'Might as well, whilst I can. You too, Mark.'

So the Captain climbed into his bed and the man into his straw pallet, and for a while they both slept. But presently Mark was woken by a hand shaking his shoulder gently. He sat up quickly, his eyes open, his mind alert.

It was Drake, swathed in a thick, dark cloak, his eyes shining with excitement.

'Swiftly, Mark. The clouds race across the moon, for a fair wind has got up. But I think we must leave our post for a little.'

Mark hurried out on deck to find the rustle and murmur of subdued activity all around—and the guiding lantern no longer burning. He turned, bewildered, to an officer standing near by who recognised him in the drifting moonlight as Drake's servant.

'Look lively, fellow,' he said with a smile. 'Here's a chance of some fun for us and no loss to any but Philip of Spain! Our commander (who has the sharpest eyes in the fleet, I'll wager) has caught a glimpse of something that needs investigation. It may be a simple vessel owned by some neutral power—or perhaps a Spanish galleon which is trying to steal past us in the darkness so that it can fall upon us in the morning.' He chuckled at the open astonishment on Mark's face. 'Or it may be the *Nuestra Señora del Rosario,* trying to repair her injuries and, therefore, an easy pigeon for the plucking,' he ended.

As Mark hurried about his duties in the freshening north-easterly breeze, he found himself filled with a mixture of heady excitement and horrid doubt. Was it sensible to steal away after a possible prize, when the whole fleet looked to their light for guidance? Then the ship began to gybe as softly as a whisper, and they bore down upon the unsuspecting Spanish galleon, as it undoubtedly was, whose crew were making so much clamour as they tried to rig a jury-mast by the fitful moonlight that they were unaware of the English vessel until she was within musket shot.

After that, there was little excitement. The Spaniards were in no condition to fight, nor to run. When they heard the name of Sir Francis Drake, they were eager enough to surrender, and the commander of the ship, Don Pedro de Valdes, was brought on board the *Revenge*, for he would bring them in good ransom money.

They had met with the barque *Roebuck* in the darkness, and it was she to whom Drake entrusted his prize, to be taken into Dartmouth. Having been missing from the fleet for eighteen hours, they crowded on all canvas to get back to their rightful position. Then Mark rowed in his usual place in the galley across to the *Ark Royal* with Drake and his noble prisoner, and, far from censuring their conduct, the Lord Admiral was pleased that already a prize had been taken, with the additional (and much needed) titbit of twenty-eight battery-guns and ammunition.

'Some are not so pleased,' Drake said with a chuckle in the privacy of his cabin as Mark helped him out of the formal garments he had donned to visit the Admiral of the Fleet. 'Apparently when dawn broke this morning the fleet were a trifle scattered because they had lost sight of the lantern. Old Frobisher is bellowing like a bull at the thought that I should get prize money where he will get none. Poor fellow, he's notoriously unlucky with prizes. But with so many fat Spaniards about, my Martin must get one for himself, and not expect me to catch a small fortune for him.'

'You'll sleep now, sir?' said Mark hopefully. He had managed to get only a couple of hours' rest himself the previous night and realised that with each succeeding day the battles would grow more desperate. Drake nodded, smiling to himself as at some private joke.

'Yes, better sleep whilst we may,' he remarked, throwing himself down upon his bed and settling his head on the pillow. 'For they won't like having lost one of the bigger galleons to us so early in the engagement—to me, particularly. It's said that Philip has a particular hatred for me, though I'm sure I don't know why ...' His voice trailed away and Mark saw that Sir Francis slept at last, but still the smile lingered, impishly, round that determined mouth.

★ ★ ★ ★

On land, excitement and determination to make the Spanish pay dearly for every foot of English soil they invaded kept an atmosphere of high tension everywhere, but never more so than in the coastal towns of England.

As the Armada travelled through the Narrow Seas, the beacons, one by one, blazed their warning at night and smouldered it thickly by day. People grew closer than they had been in living memory, the market woman not thinking twice about stopping the grand lady to ask for news of the battles, for did they not both have men who were defending their lives at sea, or preparing to do so on land?

Most people knew that the fleet were desperately short of powder and shot. Folk melted down their cooking pots, wrought-iron railings, anything. Then they shaped them into cannon balls and crept down to the little boats, to pull softly away in the dark of the night, find the fleet, deliver the precious shot, and row home again the next night. Women baked big flat loaves of bread and sent them in the small craft, with now and then a few cabbages or apples to help the diet of men who, they knew, were fighting with empty bellies and little hope of extra aid from the Treasury.

Other men drilled and practised man-oeuvres, the younger ones amongst them hoping that they would be given a chance to show their prowess, the older, wiser ones praying that they would not.

And the Queen, as if to show her people that she would be with them in body as well as in heart and mind, went down at the height of the danger of invasion, with rumours running rife that Parma's troops were even then crossing the Channel, to review the troops at Tilbury.

'Amongst all those crowds she will go, whatever we say,' commented Burghley bitterly. 'A stray shot, a quick and silent arrow—even a knife, for she gets so close to her people—could do more harm to this country than if every English ship was destroyed. For it is *she* for whom the men fight; *she* who inspires the love of her people and the hatred and envy of Spain. But nothing will stop her. She laughs in my face. "An assassin? Always someone warns me of an assassin," she tells me. Then she reminds me (as if I need reminding) that her own Admiral of the Fleet, Lord Howard, is a staunch Catholic and if he will take a major role against the Spaniards what would some other, lesser, Catholic want to kill her for?'

'She has no thought of her own danger—never has had,' agreed Leicester, to whom the older man had spoken. 'God, Burghley, if ever she had not lived in danger of her life, it was before I knew her—and we played together as children.'

'Her presence will make the whole nation determined to fight as never before,' promised Walsingham. 'God, who would have believed a woman could command such love and such loyalty? She'll walk amongst the troops and every time she smiles, thirty humble peasants will think "The Queen has smiled on me!" and will fight like a man possessed, for a woman he had heard of all his life, and has seen perhaps for the first time.'

'Well, news from the fleet is good; they seem to have the whip hand over Philip's precious Armada. And the rumours of Parma setting out with his invasion fleet may well be false.'

But the words were not spoken with

210

much conviction and throughout the length and breadth of England tension and determination alike mounted. The Spanish and Parma's hardened troops might come—but what a reception would meet them!

★ ★ ★ ★

Like the others, Liza could only wait and pray, and prepare herself as best she might for whatever came.

Then, on 15th August, she had a message from her husband. He wanted her to ride to London immediately to the small inn where he was staying, because he did not fancy the lonely comforts of lodgings without her.

They met eagerly, and Liza searched his face for signs of despair. But she read there only tiredness and relief from fears.

'I should probably still be pursuing the Armada, but real gales have blown up and our fleet got scattered. A number of our ships managed to stay in formation and are making sure that the Spaniards continue to fly before the wind, but the *Revenge* had to put in to harbour, and here I am, with despatches of course.'

'My darling, I'm so glad you're safe!' cried Liza, her eyes filling with tears of relief. 'Is our danger over now? Would it be possible for Parma's force to set out across the Narrow Seas?'

'We are safe enough: the Armada will not—could not—turn and attack. As for Parma, he'll have dispersed his troops by now, according to our spies. He never had the faith in the "Enterprise of England" that he pretended to Spain.'

'Did we lose many men? How did the Spanish fare?' asked Liza.

'We lost few men, and the galleons are cut down to size, their sails torn by wind and cannonball, their sides battered by our broadsides. Men died like flies aboard their troop-carriers. What chance had they, when the shot raked the decks? They died because they were packed too close. When it caught the vessels amidships, they died in their quarters. But I'll tell you the tale when you're washed and fresh and can sit down to a decent meal.'

But he would not begin his story until the main courses had been eaten. Then, with the fruit bowls on the table and the cutlery which had been unused also lying on the board, he began.

'We fought the first big battle off the Isle of Wight, with the loss of only a few men. By God, but we realised then that Spaniards though they might be, they were going to make us fight for our victory! We had already taken a prize of course, the *Nuestra Señora del Rosario,* but no vessel had been sunk in battle. Nor was, at that time on either side.'

He tipped fruit unceremoniously out of the bowls and cluttered the sharp fruit knives into a heap.

'Look, I'll use these like a sort of movable map, to show you how the battles went. See these apples? They'll be the big galleons which the Spaniards guarded most devotedly. Their fighting formation—well, you saw that off Plymouth—was a crescent, the horns of which were about seven miles apart. The galleons were fighting formation here—' He slid the apples smoothly across the polished table top. 'Over here was the English fleet.' Sharp knives moved under his hand. 'The Spaniards fought well, yet we would have had them then instead of later, had it not been for lack of powder and shot. Do you know, at one stage of the battle we melted down our anchor chains for cannon balls?'

He ground his teeth, then he smiled apologetically. 'No use fretting now, but I can tell you we fretted then! The worry and anxiety lest we had to withdraw from battle for lack of powder and shot—such a *petty* reason, Liza! However, back to the battle. See this big apple—galleon, I mean? It was the *San Mateo* and two of our ships fell upon her suddenly, causing her to fall back. She turned into the other galleons—' The apple skated round like a wood in a game of bowls and clunked softly against the fruit crowded on either side of it. 'And they—the Spaniards—had to manoeuvre as quickly as their bulk would allow to avoid a bad collision. They were close to the sandbanks just off the Isle of Wight, yet hemmed in by the cliffs of the island, and we thought we had them beat. But Howard knew we were perilously close to running out of ammunition. We had poured broadside after broadside into the galleons, far more powder and shot than had been calculated when we were first munitioned, because we were never allowed to use live ammunition in our training manoeuvres. So now the galleons came to the best order they could and leaving behind the *Santa Anna* and three galleasses—abandoned to sink or struggle as best they might—they headed all unknowing for Seymour, who lay in wait for them in the Narrow Seas with his fleet.'

'Sir George Carey saw the battle from the island,' Liza told him. 'He half-guessed why you suddenly stopped fighting; he thought the Spanish must also have been short of powder and shot.'

Drake shrugged. 'It's possible. But it was an ideal chance for them to escape. There they were, pinned between the cliffs of Shanklin and the sandbanks, yet we had to watch them go. But we followed them, and imagine our astonishment—and delight—when we realised they were swinging into the Calais roads, away from England.'

He outlined the French coast with long-stemmed roses from a convenient pot of the flowers standing on the low windowsill, and grouped his apples close, with the knives now hovering on two sides, the coast on the third, and the only passage of escape northwards.

'When night came, we were joined by Sir Henry Seymour and his fleet. A worthy addition, and just at the right moment. It should have struck dismay into the hearts of those foolish Spaniards, yet they did nothing.

'Howard called a council of war, Wynter proposed fire-ships, and it was decided to send Sir Henry Palmer to Dover, where a fleet of small vessels had been prepared for just such an occasion. However, I pointed out that Palmer could scarcely be back with the fire-ships before morning, and God alone knew when that fool, Medina Sidonia, would realise the perilous position he had chosen to anchor! The fierce, sweeping tides, the undertow, sandbanks and currents of the Calais roads are famous—or infamous, I should say. I volunteered to give one of my ships, the *Thomas*, and seven other captains handed over their vessels. We left the guns loaded and primed, for we wanted to create utter confusion.'

'But didn't Medina What's-his-name realise what was happening?' asked Liza, her forehead wrinkling in perplexity. 'Surely he must have seen the lights being kindled a good way off?'

Drake chuckled. 'So he would have, if they had been kindled a good way off. But we decided to man the ships, and to tow longboats behind them, so that the fires need not be started until the vessels were bearing down upon the Armada. Then the men would abandon their blazing beacons and row to safety.'

He paused to arrange eight scarlet cherries in a small group.

'There you are, the fire-ships. Everything went well; nothing could have been better, in fact. The men worked like demons without a whisper, the ships passed by us in the dark like a deeper darkness; nothing more. Then when they were within minutes of colliding with the Spanish fleet, a tiny spark! We saw by the glow men tumbling into the longboats and rowing hard for our craft. The Spaniards were hysterical with fear. It must have seemed to them that the devil himself was at the helm, for they could not have realised the ships were manned right up to the last moment—and then, of course, the guns began to go off.'

He cuffed the cherries, sending them bowling into the apples, and began scattering the apples with his other hand.

'We could hear the screams of fear, the friars of the Inquisition praying for help against the devil who had come amongst them with his fiery ships. Then they panicked completely. Some were in such a hurry to fly from the terror of the fire that they cut their cables and left their anchors behind them. Others collided in the darkness and were swept away north-eastwards on that strong tide. The Spanish Admiral of the Fleet kept cool enough, and tried to rally his sheep, poor, blue-blooded old shepherd! But they would not or could not obey his commands. They drove on to the north-east and Sidonia had perforce to follow instead of to lead.

'We waited until they had formed up in some sort of huddle, and fell upon them. It was broad daylight by now, of course. We dared not fire until we had drawn close, for our ammunition was still terribly, dangerously short. Yet we fought them every way save the way they wanted: there was no grappling and no boarding. It would have been suicide, for though badly injured, they were a long way from dead. They must have outnumbered us even then by many thousands, and their ships were all intended for warfare, or hospital ships, or victualling vessels. Many of our fleet were little more than cockleshells, hired or begged or borrowed from inshore fishermen by youngsters who longed to fight for their country—or older men who had sons enslaved for life in the Spanish galleys. To tell the truth, they got devilish in the way at first, but they were full of courage, every man. Full of courage.'

He was silent for a moment and Liza, turning her eyes from the table to look into his face, thought she saw the glint of tears in his eyes. Then he brought up a fresh squadron of knives and said almost brusquely, 'At the height of the fighting, Lord Howard and his ships suddenly joined us. What a ghastly shock it must have been for the Spaniards! We'd had four hours of the hardest, bloodiest fighting you can imagine. You've heard people say "the scuppers ran with blood", but one galleon, the *San Juan*, was vomiting blood from her portholes. I saw it with my own eyes, a terrible sight and one I hope never to see again.'

'You say Howard *joined* you? I thought he led, Sir Francis?'

'Ah, yes, but he'd gone off after a galleasse which the cursed commander beached deliberately. Mind you, the men plundered her on the shores of Dunkirk, until the French drove them off. It—

delayed things. But who knows? Perhaps it was for the best. The *Ark Royal* at the head of her squadron sailed into battle when we were beginning to tire. But she was fresh as paint with music playing, clean decks, alert sailors, and ammunition.'

'But surely Howard shouldn't have been prize-hunting whilst men fought and died?' said Liza indignantly.

Drake shrugged, his cheeks reddening a little. He had not mentioned his own slight defection in pursuit of the *Nuestra Señora del Rosario.*

'Anyway, we really thought that at last we had them at our mercy. Then the wind changed. No, I shouldn't say changed. A squall came across the water and before you could say knife we had to forget our guns and see to our sails. Men raced aloft, taking in the canvas. The Spanish were at the mercy of the elements, and by the time the squall had passed on, they were in shoal water.'

He pulled the long-stemmed roses into a new position to indicate the Armada's danger and, suddenly remembering, knocked a number of apples off the table.

'Out of the game—I mean battle—a lot of them. Sunk, torn apart on the shoals or driven on to sandbanks. We thought we had them without raising a finger then, Liza. God seemed to be going to do our work for us, and let us save our ammunition. The wind was strong and the sea rising. It seemed certain that they would break their backs on the shoals and England would be safe—and rich, for we could claim the broken galleons as prizes when the weather lifted.

'But the wind played us false. It veered suddenly to the south and Sidonia knew better by now than to delay. He gybed and his fleet joyfully followed him. They ran ahead of the wind up the North Sea, with Howard and his squadron and me with mine closely following to see that they didn't try to return. We thought at first they might make for Scotland, but the wind veered again; a fickle lady, our English weather, eh, Liza? We wondered if they might try to return to Dunkirk to rendezvous with Palma's invasion force, but we had taken prisoners. They assured us that not a ship was free from disease, and few were seaworthy. Most had cut their cables in Calais roads, so could anchor nowhere.

'Then the wind strengthened, carrying

the pot-bellied, torn craft mercilessly before it. They were still flying where the wind carried them, those that weren't wrecked off the coast of Scotland and the Netherlands. It's plain enough that now they'll simply skirt the Orkneys and Ireland and run for home. A pity we couldn't have finished them off, though.'

He scattered the apples across the table, grinning like a boy, then began replacing them in the ornate fruit bowls. He gathered up the knives neatly, saying, suddenly grave, 'Sickness is worse amongst the English seamen than it has ever been before. Yet no men ever fought more nobly, Liza. Not one of our sips was lost, only a hundred men killed. Yet I fear there will be a dreadful reckoning, for the bad beer, sour wine and skimped rations meant unbelievable hardships were endured by men whose bellies flapped against their backbones.'

'When will our ships return to Plymouth?' asked Liza. 'Shouldn't we be there, Frank, to give what help we can? We have had our mead of praise from the Queen and others, should we not now do our best for the sailors?'

'You are my own kind girl,' Drake said,

beaming. 'But it will have to be at our own expense, for the Queen will not hear of parting with another penny. We'll ride for Plymouth tomorrow, although the bulk of the fleet have landed at Margate and the sick are dying on the waterfront there, they say.'

But Liza was thinking of Mark, who was still on board the *Revenge,* and of Belle, who carried his child and must be getting near her time. She was thinking of the brave, laughing-eyed men who had set off from Plymouth to save their country; who now, maybe, would crawl out of their vessels at Sutton Pool and perhaps fall dead on the cobbles, whilst their wives and sweethearts could only weep. Her husband, by his very presence, could give comfort few others had it in their power to offer. He should do so.

★ ★ ★ ★

In the weeks that followed, Liza was not the only woman who toiled uncomplainingly to halt the sickness which had spread like wildfire through the fleet. But sometimes all their efforts seemed useless. A man would pull himself on to the quay, utter a faint, hoarse shout of triumph, and fall with sickening slowness to the ground, to die within hours. Some were nursed back to health in the canvas tents pitched like hospitals on the Hoe, but many more died. Some said the figure of the dead reached five thousand before the disease cleared.

Liza, sick with the smell of putrefying flesh, faint with fatigue, giddy from lack of sleep, hardly heard Belle at first. Then the voice she remembered so well came to her through her preoccupation.

'The worst of the sickness is over now, Lady Liza, and you must rest. You've done your fair share and more; now you must rest or you'll be ill yourself. Now come with Belle and let's get you tidied up and into a good, soft bed. Sir Francis is coming home tomorrow and he will want you to receive him kindly, for he has worked as hard as you, labouring for the sick sailors.'

Liza allowed herself to be led home, through streets cleaned from the victory bonfires that burned night after night, despite the terrible sickness amongst the sailors. She undressed slowly and submitted to Belle washing her thoroughly. Then she let Belle help her into bed, though she said in a sleep-thickened voice, 'It's not right that you should be lifting me in your condition, Belle. Why, you've worked as hard as I have and you might give birth at any moment by the look of you!'

It was not until Liza woke, refreshed, the next morning that Belle told her the child she carried would never know its father. Mark had been struck down with the sickness whilst still at sea.

'I did not even see his dead face,' Belle said calmly, with only the slightest tremor in her voice. 'He was buried at sea, of course, so that I feel more disbelief than the grief which would otherwise have overwhelmed me.'

Liza gave a little cry of pity, but Belle shook her head. 'Don't feel sorry for me yet, milady. It is only my mind and not my heart that admits Mark is dead.'

10

FIRST FAILURE

They went home again, to Buckland Abbey, taking Belle far from the sights and sounds of Plymouth which had begun to assume nightmare proportions in both women's minds.

Within a few days, though, Drake had ceased to be content to stroll his beloved acres, watch the fine crops growing on his land, the tithe barn steadily filling. He had bought a house in Dowgate with some of his prize money (or, rather, leased it for seventy years) and he wanted to go back there; to the heart of the action. The city of London.

And suddenly, for the first time since her marriage, Liza wanted to go home to Combe Sydenham. To have her mother near her, to see her father and her cousins. To be simply a member of a family again, instead of the mistress of a great estate and wife of a famous man. Also, Belle's time was near. Liza believed that it would be better for her friend to give birth to her child in the place where they had both been brought up instead of at Buckland, where all Belle's thoughts must stray to her dead husband.

So Drake accompanied his wife and her servants to Sydenham Castle, and went on to argue his latest case with the Queen and Council. Liza greeted her mother with tolerant affection and her father with more warmth. She was soon the petted daughter of the house once more, going on visits to see relations and friends, taking Belle gifts from the Castle gardens (for Belle was staying at her own mother's small cottage), and making a fast friend of young Geoffrey Sydenham, who was learning estate management from her father.

'But I'd sooner go to sea with your husband, cousin Liza,' Geoffrey told her wistfully. 'Mind, I wasn't inactive whilst he was dealing with the Armada. I drilled soldiers on the village green and then marched them to Yelverton for the muster. But to go to sea! It must be wonderful.'

'Many men died of sickness after the defeat of the Armada,' Liza reminded him gently. 'That is why poor Belle is here alone, to have her baby. Her husband never even set foot ashore, but was cast, dead, into the ocean.'

'There is talk of another Armada being sent from Spain,' interrupted Geoffrey, his eyes shining with youthful ardour. 'If another such *should* come (although I'm sure I hope it won't, since you look so fierce, cousin!), I shall sail with the fleet.'

'Drake is in London even now, discussing how best to prevent another "Enterprise of England", as they so boastfully called their fat ships,' Liza told the lad. 'But much though I pray it will never happen, one must never shut one's eyes to possibilities. My husband feels he must keep the Queen alert, or next time the outcome might be different.'

'If there *is* a next time, I shall be with the fleet,' said Geoffrey, tightening his lips mutinously. 'I mean to be a soldier, or possibly an explorer—a sailor, too, of course. I'm a younger son, you know, and I've no learnings towards the Church. My father would like to see me established here, as your father's bailiff. Uncle George has said he'd be glad to employ me to look after his estates. But I feel such a task is for later, when I'm old. Now that I'm young and strong, now is the time for adventure! And then I might make my fortune, might I not, cousin? Many a man has sailed with Drake poor and returned rich!'

But Liza would only laugh and turn the conversation. For a time, she wanted to forget wars, voyages—yes, even treasure. It all seemed empty and hollow after the terrible sickness she had seen amongst the very men who had saved England from the Spanish conquistadors.

Belle's time came, and Liza was with her, gripping her hands as the other girl strained to bring the child forth. With humble awe, she saw the small, dark-haired head slide slowly from between Belle's taut thighs; saw the almost abrupt emergence of the wet and bloodied body, and heard the first mewling cry as the midwife administered the customary sharp slap.

She held the new little boy whilst the midwife delivered the afterbirth, then handed him over with some reluctance to be cleaned and swaddled. She saw Belle's face—worn, white and hollow-eyed, but there was a contentment in those eyes that had never been there before.

When Belle took her son in her arms and looked into the pink and crumpled face, with the eyelids swollen from the strain of being born and the unknown light, Liza felt tears prick behind her eyes.

'He could be my Mark, couldn't he, milady?' Belle's voice was low and tired, a strange mixture of wistful longing and content.

Liza had noticed the resemblance at once and hoped that Belle would not. The child at the moment of birth was a little miniature of poor, dead Mark. But as she saw Belle holding the baby so lovingly against her full, white breasts, she knew this resemblance was one that would bring Belle pleasure, not pain. Some women might resent such a reminder. For Belle, it would bring added joy whenever she saw her son.

'Let me hold him again, before I go,' Liza begged, but the sudden widening of Belle's eyes and the way she tightened her hold on the swaddled body made her add quickly, 'Belle, I—I saw him born. I love him so, I would never harm him. It's just that he is so sweet to feel in one's arms.'

When Belle relaxed and nodded, she held the warm down of his head against her lips, and felt the pulse leap up and down in the soft centre of his cranium. She touched his skin—softer than velvet—and stroked his tiny, clenched fist. Then she gave him back to his mother, kissed Belle's cheek, and left them together.

As she rode slowly homewards, she realised that she envied Belle that palpitating scrap of humanity. She had not before given much thought to a child. She had taken it for granted after the first year of her marriage that, like Drake's first wife, she would not become pregnant. But now she realised that she had reached a stage in her development when something within her craved a child of her own. Someone to give all the warmth of her love to when Sir Francis was away on the high seas, or at Court, cajoling the Queen into agreeing to a new plan.

When she reached the castle and swung down from her mare, her arms felt empty and her breasts ached. For the first time, she felt resentment against her husband for his failure to get her with child. She entered the hallway slowly, feeling sick and bereft because she had realised her own need and had blamed Drake, unfairly, for even if he could not give her children, it was no fault of his own.

But she was jerked from self-analysis by her mother's maid who came running down the stairs, saying in a vexed voice, 'Miss Elizabeth—or should I say Lady Elizabeth—come up to your room at once, do. That black girl you brought with you is as much use as a cat with kittens—always off on some mischief of her own when she's needed. As Belle cannot serve you, your mother has told me to see that you are freshly dressed and made pretty as can be, for she has visitors.'

Liza, chuckling at being treated as a child, said meekly, 'Yes, Kynaston. Certainly, Kynaston. But I've only muddied my petticoats a little by playing at leapfrog with the village boys, and my hair is scarcely tangled at all, in spite of the kerchief in blind-man's-buff.'

'You may have your fun, Miss, but that gown is not your best, and there's blood on the sleeve of your shift,' pronounced her mentor firmly. 'Why you ever brought that little blackamoor amongst decent Christians is more than I can understand, for all she ever does is trot out of the house to get amongst the men in the stables.'

'Rose is a charming child, though over-fond of men,' admitted Liza, unfastening her bodice and allowing Kynaston to ease her out of it. 'But you haven't asked me whether Belle has given birth.'

'Knew she had the moment you walked in. You wouldn't have left, otherwise,' said the older woman crossly, but her eyes softened. 'Was it a boy?'

'Yes, funnily enough it was. How did you guess?'

'Oh, just the old saying, "A life for a death". Seemed only justice that if poor young Isabelle had to lose her man, then the child should be a lad, to look after her when she grows older.'

Liza jerked crossly away from Kynaston's hovering fingers and went across to where her gowns were hanging.

'It's nonsense to talk like that. Horrible, too. The baby was growing in Isabelle's stomach months before Mark went to sea.'

'Yes, but it probably became a boy when its father died, Mistress Liza.'

Liza sighed. There was no answer to that. To change the subject, she said brightly, 'I'll wear the straw satin gown over a spangled primrose kirtle. There

233

are matching sleeves somewhere—ah, here they are. And I'll wear a fan-shaped ruff instead of the full circle. It's still too hot for the time of year.'

'Your hair, milady? Your jewels?'

'Hair I'll wear piled on top of my head, with the gold threadwork caul over it. And I'll wear the gold-and-enamel daisy chain—it winds three times round my throat and one circle falls to my waist. Pretty, isn't it?'

'Yes, it is lovely,' agreed Kynaston. 'You should look respectable enough even for the pernickety lot down there tonight.'

'Who are we entertaining, then?' asked Liza absently.

'Sir William and Lady Elizabeth Court-enay, and a more particular and pernickety lady you couldn't find,' condemned Kyn-aston roundly. 'Now will you stand still, Miss, whilst I fasten this dratted ruff?'

Liza had jumped involuntarily at the sound of the Courtenay name. Now she relaxed. He could not have known that she would be at her childhood home, therefore his call would be merely a social one.

Nevertheless, because it was expected of her, she told herself, she took all the care she could over her appearance, so that when she entered the big parlour half an hour later, the sight of her made Sir William catch his breath, whilst Lady Courtenay bit her lip with vexation.

'How charming to see you again, Lady Elizabeth, Sir William,' said Liza gaily, leaning to give the older woman the conventional Elizabethan kiss of greeting and noticing that Lady Elizabeth was pregnant once again.

Sir William clasped her hands with false fatherliness, praising her on her looks, and Liza, wrenching herself away from his grasp with a heightened colour, said quickly, 'I'm glad to see you both well.'

'Where is your husband, Lady Elizabeth?' put in Lady Courtenay waspishly. 'Doubtless dancing attendance on the Queen after the success of the victory of the Armada.' Her laugh was bitter and affected.

'I hear you did well out of the Armada, sir,' said Liza quickly, turning to Sir William. He responded easily and without embarrassment for his wife that though he had not sailed with the fleet, he had done better than some.

'A ship from the fleet was wrecked on my land—a place called Hope Cove. I got

235

a deal of prisoners to ransom.'

'A ship of war, Sir William? Or one of the fleet carrying treasure?' said Liza wickedly, knowing full well that the vessel had been a hospital ship and that reports had it that Sir William had treated his Spanish prisoners none too well, despite his carefully concealed Catholic leanings.

Fortunately, perhaps, his wife came to his rescue with a long, grumbling tale of how they had to supply clothes and food for the nobler men aboard her, so that they would be doubly glad of the ransom money when it arrived.

'Indeed, we shall have earned it,' she said, nodding her head and folding her hands complacently over her extended stomach.

Under cover of the conversation, which now became general, Sir William asked Liza how long she would be staying with her parents.

'I rejoin my husband at Buckland Abbey for the Christmas holiday,' she told him. 'He is in London at the moment, discussing the affairs of the Navy with the Queen. But everything grinds to a halt for Christmas and the New Year, and even Sir Francis will devote his energies to enjoyment instead of work.'

'Maybe I'll ride over to see you,' said Sir William thoughtfully. 'Whatever Sir Francis is planning this time, I'll be bound there will be profit in it. I could do with some money—who could not, indeed? Of course, the battle against the Armada was different. I wonder, now, could Drake be considering a raid on the Spanish treasure fleet?'

'I never know what he intends,' said Liza with assumed indifference and complete untruthfulness. 'But surely you wouldn't want to go a-venturing with your wife in her present condition?'

He shrugged and turned to look at Lady Courtenay. Liza thought appreciatively that he was no whit less handsome than when he had smiled on her during her youth. His face was given a slightly devilish look, certainly, by his slanting eyebrows, and his lips when they smiled had a sarcastic twist. But his shoulders beneath the dull red satin doublet were broad despite the padding and not merely because of it, his waist was still narrow, and his legs as strong and shapely as they had always been.

'Have I changed, Liza?' he said smoothly,

and Liza found herself colouring, for she had been sure he was unaware of her scrutiny.

'You've aged, of course,' she said sweetly, unable to resist the small scratch at his self-esteem. 'But otherwise—no, you are very much the man you were.'

'Still my spirited lass,' Courtenay said approvingly, and was rewarded by the sparkle of annoyance in her eyes as she turned on him, saying quickly, 'Never *your* lass, Sir William. Nor would I have been.'

The party began to marshal themselves to go in to dinner, and Sir William had, perforce, to hover round his wife, whose eyes had seldom left him during his quiet talk with Liza.

But after dinner, in the evening hush, when Lady Elizabeth Courtenay had been packed into her coach and sent off up the drive, Sir William said softly, 'Ah, how I've regretted that I let you slip out of my grasp when we were at Court together, Liza. I could have plucked you like a rose, you would have known how strong an ardent man's love can be. But I was a ward of court and married where I was bid. You in your turn had to submit to the rich and famous sea-captain. But he has not yet got you with child, and surely a warm-hearted girl like you wants children?'

'There is time for a family,' said Liza airily. 'I married Sir Francis because I loved him, not because he was rich or famous.'

They were standing close together in the courtyard whilst his horse, tethered to the side of the mounting block, shifted impatient hooves. Liza's parents had called goodnight and gone indoors, leaving their daughter to take her leave of the friend of her youth. Knowing them, she guessed they were already in their bedchamber, drowsily getting undressed.

'Your horse is impatient,' Liza said, feeling that the silence had suddenly become overcharged with meaning.

'I, too, am impatient.'

Unexpectedly, Courtenay put his hand on her stomach, pressing hard with his fingers so that she could feel the movement even through the stiff boning of her bodice. She became aware of a deep feeling of pleasure coursing through her veins; intermingled with guilt, certainly, but nonetheless enjoyable for that. Afterwards, she thought she should have stepped back sharply, or even slapped his face. At the time, she did neither. Her breath came fast, her heart seemed to be pounding all over her body, and for the first time since her marriage she knew hot and urgent desire for a man other than her husband.

Sir William seemed to sense it. He pulled her close to him, shamelessly kissing her lips, her eyelids, her forehead. She did not respond, but neither did she pull back. She stood in his arms, a victim of her own weakness.

'I could give you a child,' he murmured in her ears. 'Women quicken with me, Liza. You may not burn with desire for me as I burn for you, but you want a baby, don't you? I can tell when a woman wants to feel she is fully a woman, her belly swollen with child.'

Liza felt faint and giddy, surprised both by her own feelings and by his perspicacity, which had seen and understood her longing, before she had more than half-acknowledged it to herself. She drooped against his chest, suddenly submissive, and if he had picked her up and carried her into the stable, to make love to her on the piles of hay like any common dairymaid, she would not have resisted him.

But even as his grip tightened to swing her off her feet, a figure emerged round the side of the house. Humming airily, white teeth gleaming in her brown face, Rose called a polite greeting.

Liza heard Sir William say 'Damn!' viciously beneath his breath, before he released her so suddenly that she lurched and almost fell.

Realising now that she must escape with what dignity she could muster, Liza said, 'Wait Rose. I'm just bidding Sir William farewell. We will go upstairs together.'

Rose, fresh from the arms of her latest conquest, had little time or desire to speculate on the lives of others. She waited obediently at the foot of the stairs, therefore, seeing Courtenay swing himself into the saddle of his roan stallion.

But she didn't hear his parting words to her mistress.

'Another time, my pretty,' he called softly as Liza turned to go into the house. 'Don't forget, there'll be another time.'

'Not if I know it,' Liza said viciously, biting her lower lip with sharp white teeth. She hadn't realised she had spoken aloud until she saw the pleased smile disappear from Rose's face, to be replaced by doubt.

What, Rose thought, had she done wrong this time? For once she was where she should be, ready and waiting to help her mistress to bed.

'I only spoke my thoughts aloud, Rose. Come along now, it's late and you must be as tired as I am.'

But when she lay in her bed, Liza was unable to sleep. She turned restlessly, scooping the blankets over her ears, then pushing them back so her shoulders were bare. I behaved like a whore, she thought, shocked. I'm a weak and foolish woman who does not see enough of her man. It is true that I want a baby, but truer, if I must face facts, that this evening I wanted what Courtenay was offering. As for Courtenay himself, she should not have been surprised at *his* behaviour; he never changed. His interest in women lay only in possessing their bodies. He would be as happy to lie hip to hip with Rose as with herself. But the thought sent a stab of surprising jealousy through her; that Rose, a lonely orphan, could command the attentions of a score of men whereas she herself had to wait for Sir Francis to forget affairs of state and remember affairs of the heart.

And she knew, though she had tried to

ignore the knowledge, that more and more of late he came to her bed with no thought of lovemaking.

Now, lying alone in the bed where she had slept as the virgin daughter of Lord and Lady Sydenham, she began to face facts. Drake was a man who could live to the full without women. He loved his wife, but, especially of late, the act of love had become for him more of a duty than the rare and beautiful experience it had seemed to Liza. That he enjoyed his duty she acknowledged. But she knew that for her this was no longer enough. The preliminary loveplay which he had gradually dismissed from their bedding was necessary for her self-esteem and also, to be truthful, for her enjoyment. She was feminine enough to feel pique at the perfunctory nature of his embraces, the quick, rather embarrassed peck on the lips before he left her for several weeks. And she was woman enough to want to bear a child.

If his love for her had been all-embracing, she suddenly realised, the lack of a child would not have worried her. But he could only give what he had, and that did not fill her needs.

So she lay in her bed, staring up into the darkness of the canopy overhead, and feeling resentment against Sir Francis for his lack of understanding, and for the love which she had to share with his work.

* * * *

'Well, Frank, I wish you Godspeed and a safe return.'

Liza forced her stiff lips into a smile which wobbled uncertainly for a moment, then as she straightened her shoulders, returned with more conviction.

'You could also wish me good luck in my venture, success, and the spoils of war, Liza.'

'Oh, I do. Just take care of yourself—and of my little cousin, Geoff.' Suddenly the feeling of being left behind once more softened her resolutions. She clung to Drake's doublet, kissing him passionately, trying to forget their shared, unspoken discontent, remembering only that he was running into danger with his eyes open, for the sake of his country and for the plunder which that country needed to refill her treasure chests after the cost of the Armada.

'Will you say farewell to me with such enthusiasm, cousin Liza?'

Liza pulled away from Drake's embrace and turned to Geoffrey Sydenham, spruce and neat in maroon doublet and hose, his ruff and stockings gleaming immaculately white against the background of the side of the *Revenge*.

'A picture of the perfect sailor,' she said, laughing at him and standing on tiptoe to kiss his fresh young cheek where the down of his newly grown beard grew, soft as a cat's fur.

'Good luck, Geoff, on your first voyage. I hope you may bring home treasures enough to buy yourself manors and estates,' she said, smiling up at him. 'Don't forget me, when you're looting rich Spanish towns. I'd like ...' She tilted her head in mock consideration, dimpling, 'I'd like an emerald necklace at the very least.'

'You shall have it, since you're the only woman in my life. Farewell, cousin Liza. Think of me often.'

He picked up his box of gear and boarded the *Revenge*. A hand lifted in farewell, a smile, and he was gone. Liza turned her attention back to her husband.

'He's a nice lad. I hope he won't be

disappointed in his search for adventure. Doesn't the *Revenge* look good since she's been repainted?' Liza said, admiring the giltwork round the poop of the ship which she had last seen, tarnished and dirty, when the fleet had returned to harbour, crestfallen, because of contrary winds. All of the fleet, that is, except the *Swiftsure*, commanded by Sir Roger Williams, and carrying the Queen's current favourite, Robert Devereux, Earl of Essex.

Devereux had run away from Court like a naughty boy to join the fleet. Like Philip Sidney had done, some years earlier. But unlike Sidney, Devereux had outwitted them by actually setting sail under his friend Sir Roger. Bad weather or no, they had not returned with the rest of the fleet, and Liza thought with an inward grin that both Devereux and Williams would happily weather the worst of storms rather than return to Plymouth like whipped curs, to endure their Sovereign's undoubted wrath!

'We have not enough men for the venture, we are as usual sadly under-victualled, and we should have left months ago. But at least the additional time has meant that the ships look their best,' said

Sir Francis. His eyes searched Liza's face, and Liza knew Drake had noticed her changed attitude.

They were sailing to Lisbon with the Pretender to the Portuguese throne, Don Antonio, planning to conquer all and to place the insignificant little man on the throne in the face of all Spain! Liza, who had had to entertain the Pretender to the Portuguese throne under her roof for several months and had felt considerable distaste for his boastful, sly manners and his whining voice, could only regard such an enterprise with doubt. On the other hand, if anyone could win for Don Antonio, it was Drake. But so many things had gone wrong already! The Queen had added a Proviso to the conditions under which the fleet would sail; she was secretly convinced that Philip II was building a second Armada. Therefore, she said, Drake and Norreys (the soldier in command of the land forces) must not make straight for Lisbon, as they had arranged. They must first attack the new invading force, wherever it lay at anchor, and utterly destroy it.

'That will bring news of your presence speedily to Spanish ears—King Philip's ears,' Liza had protested. Drake had nodded wearily.

'But it's agree or be forbidden to sail,' he had said.

Now he said, with an attempt at gaiety, 'Well, perhaps it is as well that we shall set off with half the promised numbers of soldiers, no cavalry at all, and very little food. Because as you can see, we have only half the number of ships in our fleet that we were promised, so any other men or horses would have had to swim!'

'You are without the promised siege train, and the Dutch ships and soldiers haven't come as they said they would. Laugh that off,' Liza said bitterly.

'I have to; what alternative have I? Do you think that it is my wish to run into a Spanish port with insufficient men, shipping, munitions and food? But I must show no one a face of doubt, for they look to me for leadership.'

He kissed Liza brusquely. 'Pray for me,' he said. Then he was on board the *Revenge*, the gangplank was hauled up, and the fleet set off, slowly at first, then as the wind caught their sails, faster.

Superstitiously, Liza watched until they were below the horizon. Then she turned and made her way back to her home in High Street. She would soon be leaving there, to go to Buckland Abbey for a while. Then she might go to their new London house, the Herbery, with its wide, handsome rooms still lacking furniture, and the garden that sloped down to the river needing the loving hand of its mistress. She had always enjoyed gardening; planning, weeding, planting out, gathering the fruits of her labours. And at Dowgate she would be within easy reach of her friends at Court, should any wish to visit her. But first, they would go to Buckland.

They set off the next day. She and Belle, baby Mark, the erring but unrepentant Rose, and the rest of the servants. For Belle, Liza realised, the return to Buckland would be painful. Her house was finished, but she had not yet seen it; and Mark, who had planned it and done nearly all the building of it, would never see it. Even as she thought which hangings she could best spare for Belle, she knew that to furnish a house which her lover would never enter could only give Belle pain. But it would have to be faced. Belle would have to employ some good woman to look after her child and a man to work the land. She could repay them only by continuing to work as a lady's maid for a time, until the land began to pay for itself. Then they would see.

There was plenty of work to be done at the Abbey, but within forty-eight hours of their arrival Liza told Belle gently that she was going to take her home. Belle's face paled and her body, still slightly plump after the birth of her child, tensed. Then she nodded and turned away.

She showed no emotion as they stared out of the window of the coach at the house. They had decided it was better to travel the short distance in the vehicle because of the baby and because the coach could bring quantities of the hangings, blankets and bedcurtains that Liza was giving Belle for the new house.

It was a fine day and the sun shone on glittering windows and smoothly plastered white walls. They climbed out of the coach and the housekeeper Liza had installed for Belle opened the front door, then disappeared tactfully into the kitchen regions.

Belle stopped in the doorway, and ran her hand down the golden oak of the doorpost. The rich carving that decorated it swelled and curved, but never lost its smooth flowing line.

'Mark was a craftsman, wasn't he, milady? See with what loving care ...' Her voice broke and she stopped short, biting her lip, trying to prevent the tears in her eyes from spilling down her cheeks so that everyone would see that she wept.

'I'll take baby Mark for you, Belle. You go up to your room for a while,' Liza said encouragingly. 'It must hurt to see the house, my dear. It just shows how much you loved Mark. And in every piece of beautiful carving, in every foot of shining floorboard, are traces of his love for you. Now go, and have your cry out. Then we'll talk of your plans for the future.'

Belle went stumbling up the stairs, harsh tearing sobs fighting for release, and Liza carried the baby into the parlour and sat down in one of the two big chairs. She turned the child in her arms so that the light would not fall on his sleeping face, and waited.

* * * *

For once, news of Drake's voyage filtered through to Liza before he could tell her himself. Partly, it was because, after an unsuccessful attempt to take Lisbon by an overland march from Peniche, despatches had arrived from England demanding that the truant Essex return at once. He was glad enough by now to comply—he had marched for forty-five miles with Norreys and had known the discomforts of an empty belly, and had seen men die from a disease which could as easily have stricken an Earl as a commoner. So he sailed back to England with news only of failure.

Expecting her husband home at any moment, Liza moved into the Herbery. But he did not come—and when he did arrive, he went straight to the Court. Liza waited, as she knew well how to do.

Then one morning, as she sat in her parlour nervously embroidering a shirt for her husband, and picking half-heartedly at a bowl of fruit, a voice from the doorway hailed her, making her jump and turn sharply.

'So your husband is home, eh, Liza? But we don't hear much of the marvels of *this* voyage.'

Sir William Courtenay strolled into the parlour of the house as though he owned it, took a plum from the dish, and sank his white teeth into the wine-dark fruit. Above the plump curve of the glossy skin of the gage his sparkling, slanting eyes met Liza's. The expression in them was sardonic, questioning, undoubtedly affectionate.

'You shouldn't come in here unannounced,' Liza said uncertainly. She thought perhaps she had been unwise to allow Sir William to visit her as frequently as he had done during Drake's absence. But he had been a good friend when she needed one, and though he had made no attempt to hide the admiration he felt for her, he had behaved with almost exaggerated propriety.

'How much do you know about this voyage, Liza?'

She hesitated, not wanting to tell him bad news which might never become general knowledge. 'The expedition does not seem to have succeeded altogether,' she said cautiously.

Courtenay gave a shout of laughter. 'What a masterpiece of understatement,' he said gleefully. 'The ships—those that are left—limp into harbour by twos and threes, disease is rife, and not one single town was taken and held. And you say the expedition did not succeed altogether.'

'They took Coruna,' Liza said crossly.

'Only the lower town. What good was that? It was the fortifications of the upper town which should have been taken.'

Liza pursed her lips and drew her brows together as forbiddingly as she could. But her heart was sore for her husband. She knew why he wanted her in London—because he would need the comfort of her presence when he left the Court. Knowing him as she did, she realised that it was not the apparent failure of his mission (to set Don Antonio upon the throne of Portugal) that would gnaw and fret at his heartstrings. It would be the death of so many of his men. Above all else, Drake valued the lives of those whom he led. To lose men in a cause which made England the safer had to be faced, but to lose men in a lost cause—that was heartbreak, and something for which he would find it difficult to forgive himself.

Liza remembered wistfully the first time she had seen Drake. When he had come swaggering into the Ante Chamber with self-confidence glowing from his eyes and wearing a king's ransom on his back. But that had been eight years ago. He had been thirty-six, in the prime of life. He had feared no one, needed no excuse for his action. Now it was different.

At forty-four, with everything, it seemed, against him, his prodigious luck had suddenly turned sour on him. Every decision he had taken now seemed to have been the wrong one. He had been forced to guess which harbour the Armada fleet was being built up in; he had guessed wrongly. He had attacked Spanish towns and shipping and done a great deal of damage, but had failed to take Lisbon. And though no one could openly speak of it, his worst sin in the Queen's eyes would be that he had brought back no treasure for the English coffers.

'They say Fenner sailed the *Dreadnought* into Plymouth Sound with only eighteen men fit enough to help him, out of the three hundred who sailed with him,' said Courtenay.

Liza compressed her lips and bent over her sewing, but her heart jumped in her breast.

'As for the *Gregory*, she was like a ghost ship, for only eight men were still stirring on her deck as she crawled into harbour.'

'Perhaps it's only gossip,' Liza said stiffly. 'Surely things could not come to such a pass in so short a time? They've not been at sea for much over two months.'

'Already there are riots in the West Country; soldiers and sailors—those that remain alive—are marching on London, saying they've not been fed or paid,' remarked the Job's comforter beside her. 'They saw their companions die with their own eyes, and now they feel for themselves the gnawing pangs of hunger. I don't think even *you* would accuse them of imagining their wrongs.'

'If you've come to upset me and make me miserable, then you can go again,' snapped Liza, suddenly losing patience. 'For God's sweet sake, why have you pretended friendship when I was told plainly I was not welcome at Court? If it was indeed friendship, then why do you taunt me with my husband's failure now?'

'Perhaps because my friendship has not been rewarded,' said Courtenay smugly. Liza lifted her hand impetuously, burning to box his ears soundly. Then she remembered that to cause a scandal with the Courtenays was scarcely likely to help her husband; he had troubles of his own. Her hand paused, then travelled smoothly to the hood which she adjusted carefully on her dark hair.

Sir William laughed. 'I'm sorry, Liza. I shouldn't have said that. But come, be a sensible woman. These rumours have the sound of truth to me. You would hear about them soon enough, maybe in a public place where everyone would watch your face for signs of dismay and distress. Better to hear bad news in your own parlour. You may weep on my shoulder if you wish, though I thought—only for a moment, mind—that you were more inclined to give my head a good drubbing than indulge in a hearty bout of tears.'

'Thank you, Sir William,' said Liza with all the dignity she could muster. 'It was thoughtful of you to forewarn me and I'm sorry I misjudged you. But don't you think you should return to your estates soon? You've been in London for almost a month, and—and—'

'You don't want your husband further distressed by rumour. Very well, my dear. How is your maid's baby?'

Liza began to say eagerly, 'Oh, he thrives, he is eating well ...' before she saw from the meaning smile in his eyes that it was more than a random remark. He had once offered to lie with her so that she might beget a child. Afterwards, in the cold light of day, she had wondered whether she had imagined the whole incident, or whether the remark had been an odd sort of jest, in poor taste.

She looked at him doubtfully now, wondering why he could not be more straightforward. Then he said briskly, 'Well, if I'm to be off for Devon today, I'll kiss you goodbye.' Before she could do more than rise to her feet, meaning to offer him her hand, he had caught her by the shoulders and planted his mouth firmly on her lips.

She fought the rush of desire for him that made her want to throw her arms up round his neck and pull him down on top of her. She kept her body rigid and her lips unresponding, and after a moment he released her with a little laugh.

'Foiled again, eh, Liza? One of these days—but I won't bore you with promises. Just remember what I told you once—there will always be a next time.'

He threw his plum stone into the empty hearth and left the room. She heard his firm tread crossing the wide hall, descending the three stone steps into the street, and saw him pass beneath the window, one hand raised in casual farewell. Then he was gone, leaving her to face the unpleasantness that lay ahead as best she might.

11

A SPELL AT HOME

The parlour at the Herbery had been the only open observer of their meeting; they had embraced quickly and their remarks had been trivial. Liza had told Sir Francis about his lands and showed him the progress she had made on the garden. He spoke of needing new shirts, and of wanting to buy a black stallion he had seen for sale in the city.

We talk of foolish, small things now, Liza thought. But the big things will have to be faced; I cannot allow him to dodge the issue with me, his own wife. Maybe he thinks failure is not to be spoken of, to a woman. But he was pleased enough to tell me continually of his successes.

They ate, and she lay the burden of conversation on him, answering in monosyllables. He had asked no one home for the evening, so they mounted the stairs early. In their bedroom he faced her suddenly, his face and eyes pleading for her sympathy and understanding.

'Liza, my dear. To be sure, it's a bad thing for a man to be wrong. But everything was against me; the weather, our lack of equipment, even the natives who should have welcomed Don Antonio. I have been soundly rated by the Queen, my only real friend at Court, Walsingham, is dying, the courtiers and ladies snigger behind their hands as I pass. But I never thought to get an unkind reception from you.'

'But, Frank, you tell me nothing! If I had smiled on you warmly, talked freely about the estates, would you have felt the need to justify yourself to me? I don't think you would. And I'm your wife, I want to know of your failures as well as your successes. As for blame, I would never blame you. I know that given the circumstances, you probably did ten times better than any other man could have done.'

His face lit up for a second, then he turned away. 'I haven't told you the worst,' he said dully. 'Your cousin, Geoffrey Sydenham, is dead.'

'Oh, Frank!' It was a cry of pain, torn

from her at the thought of the young man whose hopes had leapt like flames before him, so that he planned to conquer the earth, reach for the stars, everything.

'I was not present when he fell,' Drake said in a low voice. 'The men were attacking Coruna, but because we had insufficient weapons and men they mined the tower, meaning to make their own gateway into the city. The attackers were too impetuous. The first half of the tower came crashing down and they rushed into the breach and were directly in line when the rest of the edifice suddenly collapsed on top of them. Geoff was killed by the falling masonry.'

'Poor lad, poor lad,' mourned Liza. 'Right at the start of the expedition, before he had known any real adventure. Oh, my poor young Geoffrey.'

'We did our best to rescue him—ten more men died in an attempt to get him from under the stones. A day and a night we tried, Liza, but it was no good.'

'God, oh, God, he lay pinned by a fallen tower, alive and in agony!' She covered her face with her hands, trying to blot out the picture of that gay young face twisted with pain and covered in the dust of fallen defences.

Drake put his arms round her, but she shrank from his touch.

'Why didn't you put him out of his misery?' she demanded fiercely. 'You would do as much for a dog! Why, why, why should Geoff have had to suffer so?'

'I couldn't order your cousin to be killed whilst there was the slightest hope of saving his life,' said Drake angrily. 'Anyway, he's dead. Men have died worse deaths, you know.'

But Liza had turned from him and was leaning out of the bedroom window, retching. It was no use knowing that others died more horribly. Geoff had been dear to her, like the young brother she had never had. She could feel his suffering with her mind and her heart; the suffering of others was different.

Much later, they lay in bed in silence, gazing wide-eyed and sleepless into the darkness. Drake had not attempted to touch her, and Liza thought with a savage bitterness quite new to her that at least he was fortunate enough to have no need of her body, or he might have felt forced to break the silence.

But in the end, her resolution proved the stronger. In a voice so low and hoarse that she scarcely recognised it, he said, 'Sweetheart, don't hold me responsible for your cousin's death. For God's sake, don't add that burden to my heavy conscience.'

Then they were in each other's arms, Liza the comforter, then Drake.

'Let us leave this city,' whispered Liza as soon as her tears were dry. 'Let us go back where we belong, to Plymouth.'

'Not to Plymouth; sickness from the fleet is still rife. We'll go to Buckland, though. Sometimes I feel old, Liza. I've had a full life, God knows, and I've felt the deck heave beneath my feet more than I've felt the steady soil of my own estates. I'm tired of begging for proper food and equipment for my men. We'll go to Buckland and take our places in the community. You can become a respectable housewife and I'll prod the pigs and watch the wheat grow. Perhaps we might even have children. You're twenty-two, a good age for starting a nursery, and if I'm with you all the time our chances of getting a child are greater.'

She agreed, smiling in the darkness at the odd thought that she kept feeling she ought to tell him, an experienced man of the world, that merely sharing a bed was unlikely to make his seed swell in her womb. He's tired, she excused him to herself. Very likely, once he's settled down at home, he'll become as virile as ever. No, more virile than ever, she corrected herself, and smiled once more to the all-seeing night.

★ ★ ★ ★

'Why was Mr Rattenbury here, Frank?'

Liza looked enquiringly at her husband, a smile hovering at the corners of her mouth. The complete landowner! she was thinking, as he strode over the strewn herbs and rushes towards her, a stout leather jerkin over his finely pleated linen shirt, and rough buckskin breeches tucked into heavy boots.

'About the water. What else should it be, love?'

Liza smiled up at him, and laid down the small gown she was laboriously stitching for baby Mark. 'You've been busy these past two years or so,' she said, laughing. 'Renting the town mills so that everyone who wants to grind their wheat into flour

265

has to pay you; yet you, the biggest wheat grower of them all, get the work done free. Bringing water to Plymouth is a charitable game, then, love? I'll bet you do very nicely out of it!'

'Landowners can't afford charity,' Drake said quickly. He was usually jovial and good tempered when Liza twitted him about his sharp business acumen, but he did not like being accused of meanness. 'Anyway, it would seem that the business is to be settled at last. The channel has been cut, the lead pipes are being laid. I've enlarged Warleigh leat so that my own mills can be built, because the lease of the town mills will soon run out.'

'Well, what further part must we take in this watering of Plymouth?' asked Liza. 'We had the fat aldermen and their wives plodding up and down the course to see whether they approved of it. My, how those fat and finely clad ladies sweated! Do you remember, Frank, we gave them a picnic lunch beside the leat, and they all watched each other like hawks before taking food, and were *so* nice in their manners. They'd unthawed by the time they got back here for dinner, fortunately, and ate our food with gusto, especially the

Saltash oysters. Finest to be had in the whole country, you told them, you rogue! As if half of them didn't have a hand in the oyster industry, one way or another. And as for the watercourse, I should think it will cost Plymouth a pretty penny, by the time you've finished it.'

'You must think of the *convenience*, my dear. I know you say I think only of watering the fleet, and it's true, of course, that pumping the water from the wells is hard and time-wasting work. But imagine the simple housewife who will no longer have to keep running to and from the wells with buckets.'

'So many wells—I wonder what will happen to them?' mused Liza. She laid down her work to count on her fingers. 'Buckwell, Finewell, Ladywell, Westwell, Quarrywell; that is five, and there are the conduits in St Andrew's Street and John Paynter's Close. They will still be used, I suppose, to carry the water?'

'Yes, and more will be built, though since Plymouth is built on rock, it should be relatively simple to use the veins of rock to chip out conduits as they did in St Andrew's and the Close. As for the wells, they'll probably be used still for fine ladies who prefer well water to the waters of the Meavy, straight from Sheepstor.'

'I shall enjoy the celebrations when the water comes in, anyway,' Liza said decidedly. 'Shall we go to our house in High Street so that we're at the centre of things? I'm really looking forward to seeing the leat fill up.'

'Yes, to be sure. But I must ride up the dry watercourse and officially open the dam, which is all that now holds back the water. You can ask some friends over for the occasion—it might be a nice gesture to ask Courtenay and his older brats. Now that he's a widower, I dare say they don't have much fun. You can ask a few well-endowed widows as well.'

'Certainly,' said Liza. 'There are plenty of people who would be interested to watch the water arrive in Plymouth. Ralegh for one, and Frobisher for another. My dear Belle and her new husband will join us, of course, Thomas and his wife—and Robert Lampen, for he planned it all.'

'Mr Lampen is a very good sort of man, but I wouldn't have said he planned it all,' Sir Francis said somewhat stiffly. 'However, he will come, of course, as one of the official party. They, naturally, will all partake of refreshments in our home.'

Liza, nodding gravely, hid her thoughts behind her solemn face. How absurd he could be over small things, this husband of hers! He did not like giving credit where the watering of Plymouth was concerned, and was always reminding people of his own part in the task and belittling the fact that the scheme had been suggested years before he had taken it up—in fact, the very leat he now claimed as 'all my own work' had been drawn up by Lampen years earlier.

However, as he grew older, Drake found it more and more difficult to take his wife's light-hearted teasing. She had spoken to him sharply once about the number of savages brought home by other sailors and abandoned in Plymouth, to die in the streets so that their burial fell upon the town's slender finances. He had shrugged his indifference, and though she had tried not to show it, she had been considerably annoyed.

To *be* a benefactor was one thing; to pose as a benefactor quite another. But she knew that where the leat was concerned she must not try to take his pride from him, so she said patiently,

'Very well love, we will entertain the officials and our friends. As you know, I enjoy entertaining.'

It was true; she *did* enjoy entertaining. But it was one thing to plan a meal carefully, giving due thought to what was in season and what would have to be brought from abroad. For friends, this was an enjoyable chore—they repaid her by their company. But she found the worthy people of Plymouth uphill work. They gaped at the cleaned street, obviously thinking Liza pernickety in the extreme to go to such lengths. They were doubtful of trying a dish that was new to them, and frequently were so bashful and ill at ease in her pleasant, well-furnished home that they were as glad as Liza when the evening was at an end.

Liza tried to be patient and understanding with them, as they thronged into her parlour and sat down at her board. But it was when the men started their interminable talk—of the sea, of the town—that she found it most difficult to play the hostess.

If she was gay and vivacious, talking and laughing, the ladies seemed quite frightened by such behaviour. So, instead,

270

she imitated them, which she found irksome; sitting quietly listening to the men's talk, occasionally showing a piece of material new to them, or a recipe which she had brought from Court.

So on the day the water was to enter Plymouth found Liza standing beside Sir William, with whom she felt more at ease than many of her other guests. He had brought his eldest daughter and his heir with him, and whilst Margaret clung fondly to Liza's hand, young William stood in an exact imitation of his father's easy stance, gazing up the dry channel.

'Well, Liza? Provided me with a few rich widows on whom to lavish my attentions?' Sir William asked in a wicked undertone as they stood waiting.

Liza jumped. Why did he always guess with such horrid accuracy, if he were not in league with the devil, she thought crossly.

As though he had indeed read her thoughts, he added, 'I'm not in league with the devil, you know. I can see stout Mrs Renthorpe, and pale and drooping Mrs Tregarren eyeing me hopefully. I know them both to be recently widowed and waiting to be snapped up by someone on the look out for a rich bride. I'm sure they'd fill my bed with pleasure, and my purse with gold. But for the moment I've a pretty little maidservant willing to do the first, and my purse would have to be slim indeed before I took one of those ladies to wife.'

'Think of the children before you speak so freely, sir,' Liza hissed. 'Or are they so used to your ways that they take it for granted when you bed with the servants?'

'They are too enchanted by the excitement of the occasion to take notice of quiet talk, and since I pay well when a girl of my household falls pregnant I suppose they know I've begot several bastards,' he said indifferently. Suddenly he chuckled, giving her an amused, sidelong glance. 'Unless they believe me to be a man of infinite charity and benevolence, of course,' he added smoothly.

Liza stifled a gurgle of laughter and was about to reply when a murmur of 'Here he comes, here comes Sir Francis!' made her stand on tiptoe to see better.

Down the leat, scarlet cloak flying in the breeze, rode Drake on his big black stallion. Behind him, almost at the horse's hooves, came the diverted river Meavy, creaming along with the surge and swirl of its passage, as dark as coffee, with foam as thick as whipped cream. A gasp went up and a wild, excited voice shouted, 'Look, even the water follows Sir Francis, like we did when we went a-venturing together. He's brought it into town at his heels, like an obedient hound.'

'Another legend to add to the store,' hissed Sir William in Liza's ear. 'But if he doesn't hurry, he'll be getting that fine cloak wet. The water really does follow fast.'

Sir Francis was well aware of it. He lingered long enough for everyone to see the phenomenon, then rode his horse out of the watercourse towards the house in High Street, whilst on every side men and women called to him. Words of love, appreciation, words tugging at his recollection of the speaker.

In the house, Liza was soon busy, trying to be a good hostess to the multitude of guests who flocked to speak to her and thank her for her hospitality.

Drake's abundant vitality and good humour seemed to overflow. He was everywhere. At her side one minute, slicing a fat capon; across the room the next, discussing the work of his mills with a landowner; pulling someone off to his study to see souvenirs of his travels.

Rose nipped neatly and quickly amongst the guests. She had a tray laden with cups of wine and was saying gaily, 'It's raining outside, good people. April showers, Sir Francis says. Those who would like to drink a cup of hot mulled wine, well spiced, to see them on their way can help themselves from my tray, or go to the master's study.'

It was, Liza, realised, a tactful way of saying the party was over. The short April evening was already on them, for when she peeped through the window she could see that the blue sky was tinted with pink and gold from the setting sun.

The light glinted on the cobbled street, wet from a recent shower. For a moment, she was drawn from the candlelight, the smell of food, the babble of sound within the house, to the peaceful evening outside. The house opposite leaned across the narrow road as though it wanted to peep at the party going on, and above its gabled roof, beaded with raindrops, she could see the swift passage of cottonwool clouds, racing gold lined before the wind.

The bowl of primroses smelling of earth

and spring suddenly smelt lovelier by far than any of the perfumes worn by the expensive women present. As the guests began to depart, Liza dragged herself reluctantly from the window, and went to Sir Francis' side to bid them farewell.

'I've asked Sir William and his lad and lass to stay for the night, and to ride out with us to Buckland tomorrow,' her husband told her quickly, under cover of a laborious speech of thanks from what surely must be the most substantial citizen (in every sense of the word) present. 'It would be a long ride home for the children, and though Courtenay assures me they would put up in some wayside tavern, I've told Rose to prepare the guest chamber.'

Liza, nodding and smiling agreement, thought sarcastically: I wager she's preparing the room! Well, if that little madam thinks she'll share Courtenay's bed whilst he's under my roof, she's mistaken. I'll not have a servant of mine whipped for a whore round Compton village for all the world to see, richly though she might deserve it.

She did not think, because she did not want to, that she had always turned an indulgent eye when Rose ran off with men before. That the sin, in this case, was more the old, foolish one that Rose, the unwanted orphan, might have what she, the indulged and petted Lady Elizabeth, might not.

Sir Francis was a hospitable man, and he insisted that his overnight guests eat a snack and have some wine before going upstairs. So it was late before Liza and Drake accompanied the Courtenays to their rooms. Stars twinkled in between the dark night clouds and Margaret was almost asleep, leaning heavily on Liza's arm as they climbed the narrow stairs together.

'You are to share Rose's little room, next door to mine, so if you wake, frightened, during the night, you can come through to me,' Liza told the small girl, leading her into the room where first Isabelle and now Rose slumbered amongst the clothes and materials. 'I'll leave a candle burning near your bed. It's only a trundle bed, but comfortable.'

Margaret smiled up at her, trying to force her eyelids to open wide. 'I'm so tired I could sleep on the floor, Lady Liza,' she said honestly. 'But what of William? Where is he sleeping?'

'Why, in the guest room, in the fourposter with your father,' said Liza, unable to resist sounding slightly smug. 'I hope he doesn't snore or kick in his sleep. I wouldn't want Sir William to be kept awake.'

She smiled down at Margaret, thinking how pretty the child looked, in her stately clothes for this 'special occasion'.

'Oh, at home Father often sleeps with people,' Margaret said guilelessly. 'Not William, of course. I think it's Biddy at the moment. She's a very pretty girl and doesn't look as though she would snore, but I dare say she kicks.' She paused, pensive. 'Father snores *and* kicks,' she went on, as Liza did not immediately answer. 'I know, because I heard Meg, who is nurse to the younger ones, telling Biddy so, when she was going to leave us for a while.'

Liza said slowly, 'I don't think you ought to tell people intimate details of your lives, Margaret. Your father would not be pleased. Now let me help you out of that dress. My, but it's very fine and grand! Crimson taffeta with gold embroidery, and the kirtle of plum-colour.'

'It's my best, for the finer months,'

Margaret said drowsily. She stretched with pleasure at the freedom from the confining bone bodice and the tickling of the stiffly starched ruff.

'I'm sorry I spoke too freely, Lady Liza. I've never done so before. I suppose it's because I'm so tired.'

'Yes, I expect so, poppet. Gracious, what a number of petticoats! Rose is helping to clear up downstairs or she would help you, for she's handier than I.'

Liza nevertheless untied strings and undid fastenings deftly, took off the farthingale of wooden hoops covered with silk, and hung the clothes carefully for the child. Margaret sat down on the bed and kicked off her satin slippers with the silver buckles. This morning the slippers had been her pride and joy; new for the occasion. Now she was more interested in the size of the blisters she was sure they had raised on her heels. She peeled off her white knitted stockings and wriggled her freed toes blissfully. Sitting on the bed in her linen shift, her hair smudged softly round her face, her straight young legs stretched before her, she looked such a child that Sir Francis, popping his head round the door, almost failed to recognise her.

Liza, tidying away the cast-off shoes and stockings, turned and smiled, saying quietly, 'She's worn out, sweetheart. I'll just settle her between the sheets and leave the candle burning by the window, then I'll leave her. I'm sure she'll sleep like a log.'

She pulled the bedclothes back and Margaret rolled between the clean sheets, sniffing their laundered freshness and smiling with pleasure.

'At home, I share my bed with Bridget and Elizabeth,' she said. 'What joy, not to have a little sister having nightmares, and waking me to fetch a drink of water. Or rolling over the edge and shrieking when she hits the floor.' She snuggled luxuriously into her pillow. 'Good night, Lady Liza.'

'Good night, poppet. Sweet dreams,' answered Liza softly. She tucked the bedclothes in and, even as she watched, the child slept.

Softly, she and Sir Francis made ready for bed. They were between the sheets when Rose tapped at the door and they saw her shadow slip softly into her own room. The door closed, and they were alone again. Liza put her hand up and drew the bedcurtains close. Despite closeting Sir William in the guest room with his son, she had not really trusted Rose not to run to someone else's side, given the opportunity. But now, all in her house were safe a-bed. Outside, the streets were quiet—so quiet that the surge of the sea could be heard distinctly. Liza fell asleep with her ears filled by the sound of the familiar waves breaking on the familiar shore.

★ ★ ★ ★

In her room, Rose lay quiet and relaxed, curled up on top of her straw pallet like a lithe young cat. When she judged the moment was right, she slipped on to the floor and opened the door without a sound. She eyed the dark mass of the big double bed. She could hear Drake's deep, rumbling breath and Liza's light, even breathing. Long experience told her that they slept and she thought without curiosity, as she glided across the room towards the outer door, that it was a long time since her master and mistress had made love. She could remember the days when she first came to England. She had had to wait for Belle to sleep, then

280

for Sir Francis to reach for his wife, and when they were occupied with each other she would run on her soft kitten's feet across their room. Now she merely waited for sleep to take them.

Outside the door, on the darkened landing, she stood still for a moment, wondering which way to go. The window had been left slightly ajar; Drake was no believer that night air killed, as were so many of the good people of Plymouth. The stairs creaked. If she went visiting young Zeb who worked in the stables she would go out of the window, and drop quietly on to the outjutting roof of the kitchen quarters.

On the other hand, Zeb did not know she would be coming to him. Once before she had visited him, and found a dairymaid before her. She stiffened like an angry cat at the recollection. The guest of the house had told her without words that he wanted her, but he had his son sleeping with him. What to do?

Even as she stood there, the door of the spare room opened slowly. Sir William Courtenay came out. He was wearing only a linen chemise and she saw his teeth flash in the dim light as he smiled at her. She smiled back, and he beckoned, pointing towards the stairs. Moving quietly towards him, she breathed, 'The third and fifth one creak. I usually go out by the window.'

'Not I,' whispered back Sir William with the ghost of a chuckle. 'Come on, Rose, we'll go down the stairs like Christians.'

They made their way down slowly, helping each other to avoid the give-away creaking stairs.

So in the end, all Liza's care was wasted.

When they returned to their respective beds as dawn was breaking, they were too tired after their lovegames to remember creaking stairs, and Liza woke, thinking the dawn chorus must have disturbed her. She turned in bed, and burrowed against her husband, hoping to wake him. But he humped his back at her, and a deep, gurgling snore began in the back of his throat.

Well, if I'm to have no pleasure, at least I know I'm not the only one, thought Liza with sleepy satisfaction. As she drifted back to sleep, Rose opened the outer door with practised softness. When Liza woke, she would never know that her wild Rose had left her young charge even for a moment during the long watches of the night.

12

THE SMELL OF THE SEA

The sun shone, clear and bright, through the bedroom window of the Herbery. Outside, even though it was still early morning, the clatter of feet on the cobbles and the shouts of cheerful people announced to Liza that another London day had begun.

The bedcurtains were thin enough to let in the light, so she slipped out of her side of the bed, making sure that she did not wake Sir Francis. He had been living in a thoroughly hectic fashion of late, she considered. He was very much in demand at Court, back in favour with the Queen, thick as thieves with old Burghley's son, Robert Cecil, and hand in glove with Ralegh.

Liza tiptoed across the room and popped her head round the door of her dressing-room. Belle was there once more—dear Belle, more friend than servant—because

283

she had a good housekeeper to look after her husband and child, and she and Liza were happy together.

Drake's flirtation with being a landowner had been a long one. Longer than he, certainly, would have wished. He had tried over and over to get the Queen's permission to sail once more, even on a private or semi-private venture. But the Queen's consistent policy seemed to be to keep Drake and his fleet at Plymouth, a sort of extra special safeguard in case the Spanish should decide to attack England and should manage to win a passage through the various English fleets which had prowled up and down the Narrow Seas these past few years.

But though the years had been shore ones for Drake, they had certainly not been quiet or uneventful. It had been Grenville who had fought to a standstill, as captain of the *Revenge,* against a great Spanish fleet, bringing many of them crashing down with his cannon. He had been foolhardy to fight against such odds, a wiser man would have withdrawn, as others of his squadron had done. But Grenville's hatred of Spain had exceeded even Drake's; and his love of fighting had exceeded any man's. So he had done great damage to what might well have been the new Spanish Armada; greater damage, in fact, than he could ever have known. For the foolhardy, brave, reckless, indomitable Grenville had refused to surrender until there was nothing of his ship left save the hull. Then mortally wounded, he had consented to being taken aboard the Spanish flagship. But even as he died, he prayed that the Spanish might not take the *Revenge* as a prize, for useless hulk though she might be, her capture would boost Spanish morale as nothing else could.

And as though Someone had heard that broken, whispered plea, a terrible hurricane had blown up. It had destroyed the *Revenge* with contemptuous ease and then turned its terrible force upon the great Spanish fleet, scattering them like chaff before the God-sent wind.

Richard Grenville's name would ring through the centuries, his exploits and the bravery with which he had faced death would be the star to lead other men on; no one would dispute that this was right. Equally, no one would remember that it had been Drake who had worked tirelessly, night and day, to get the fleet ready for sea; hoping up to the last minute that he might be included in the adventurers setting off to keep the Spanish at bay. He did not grudge Grenville a jot of the adulation his feat of endurance brought him, but Liza knew how he pined to show everyone that he, too, was still a force to be reckoned with. A man whose very name caused Spanish hearts to beat faster with fear. Yet always the Queen had held him back, to defend England should all else fail.

'Belle!' Liza's piercing whisper had her friend out of bed in a moment, eyes wide.

'Milady! Why, you're up before me. Was it the street sounds that woke you, having been away from London in summer for a while, or did you want something?'

'The noise woke me, Belle. But I do want to get up, and I don't want to disturb Sir Francis. He's spent so much time at Court, persuading the Queen to let him sail to capture treasure, or drive the Spaniards out of the French ports they've seized, or possibly go and personally burn down the Escorial with Philip II in it! So many mad schemes have been considered that now almost everything seems feasible.

But can I come into your room, then we can help each other dress?'

'Well, I'm your waiting woman on this trip, Lady Liza. But still, if you could give me a hand with my stays I'll willingly see to your dressing. That minx, Rose, is in the servants' quarters. Fetching her out would wake the dead. But why do you want to be up and doing so early?'

'Because I feel the excitement stirring in my blood, Belle, at the thought of the great city, throbbing away like a mighty heart on my own doorstep, and me lying in bed and letting it go ahead with all its early-morning business unmolested.

'I want to be out in the fine weather whilst it lasts. I want to see the Thames before the ships are as thick as the swans on the water. I want to walk down Dowgate and not be jostled and pushed by every strutting jackanapes who comes flaunting his fine feathers near my husband's house. Let's put on plain gowns, Belle, and have a bit of fun as young wenches would if they came up from the country to enjoy a day in the city.'

'Plain dresses! You'd better borrow one of mine, then, Lady Liza, for all you've brought are an array of silks and taffetas for dancing your way round the Court,' said Belle, laughing. 'Oh, I know, if you're not ashamed to be seen in your petticoat you could wear that simple flowered gown with the split in the front of the skirt and borrow my blue, low-necked bodice. Your own lawn chemise will be sleeves enough, for it's a hot day and will be hotter later, when the sun climbs.'

Within twenty minutes, the two young women were creeping down the stairs and cautiously pulling back the bolts on the door leading into the garden. The house was already astir with servants spreading fresh herbs, pounding a mound of dough in the kitchen, lighting fires for cooking, and vigorously waxing the long table before laying it ready for breakfast. Interested, indulgent glances followed the two young women as they scuttled out of the door, but no one made any comment.

After all, it was her ladyship's first visit to London for several years—certainly her first with Sir Francis once more the idol of the people. It was only natural that she should be excited, for wasn't she young yet—twenty-eight was no great age, after all, and she did not look much more than eighteen for all her careful company manners. They smiled at each other as they saw through the diamond-paned windows overlooking the garden that Liza and Belle had thrown discretion to the winds and were running hand in hand over the grass, their hair loose down their backs. Gone to feed the swans, or perhaps to get someone to row them down the Thames in the sunshine. After all, in England even in June you could never tell what the weather might do; it might rain in half an hour. The servants returned to the work of cleaning the house so that it shone, and preparing a breakfast big enough for an army, for people came visiting Sir Francis at all hours, and on a fine day they arrived early.

'Shall we go for a trip on the river, Belle?' Liza asked, glancing mischievously at the other.

Belle looked longingly at the barge which Drake had just bought. It had purple cushions with gold tassels and was fetchingly painted. It had a figurehead of a pelican (after the ship in which Sir Francis, then plain Master Francis, had circumnavigated the globe), and it was called the *Golden Hind*, just in case anyone might not realise who lounged at his ease under the canopy, or who was the owner of the coat of arms which figured prominently on the bows, and was cunningly embroidered in all its colours on the canopy.

'A sable shield, with two stars argent, the globe terrestrial with a ship under sail upon it, held by a golden cable with a hand appearing out of the clouds,' chanted Liza, who had embroidered the crest too many times to regard it entirely with the respect it deserved.

Belle, who had helped equally often with the task, finished the catalogue of the crest's intricacies. 'And a wivern caught in the rigging, arse over tip with the motto ...' She paused to giggle, and the two finished in chorus, 'Divino Auxilio, Sic Parvis Magna.'

'But you're not thinking of venturing on the river in that great thing, milady,' Belle said when they had stopped laughing. 'It needs strong men to use the oars, and I'd be ashamed to be seen on the river with my hair loose. We look like a pair of girls who have escaped from their mother for an hour, instead of two respectable married women.'

'Oh! But isn't it nice to feel the wind

in your hair, Belle? I know caps and bonnets and hoods must be worn, but in the quiet of one's own garden it's such a treat to forget convention and feel free and foolish.'

Her pleading tone made Belle smile. 'Well, when your garden ends in the river, and that river is the waterway taken by half the world, it's not exactly private, milady. Shall we stroll round the garden? You've done so well with it, and the bluebells are only now beginning to fade beneath the beech. You've some beautiful roses in bloom already, by the south wall.'

They strolled round the garden, criticising and commenting, bending to pull a weed or reaching up to test a fruit. Then they walked down to the Thames. Already the river traffic was beginning to build up. Oarsmen sculled leisurely past, probably to pick up a young sprig of the nobility who was coming home after a night enjoying the more questionable pursuits available in the city. A small boy manoeuvred his cockleshell craft neatly amongst the other vessels, whilst an even smaller girl sat in the stern, throwing pieces of stale manchet bread to the swans.

'Let's go indoors, and we can pin up

our hair and become respectable; then we can go down to the street market and buy—oh, pretty combs for our hair, ribbons, laces—anything,' Liza said eagerly, but Belle shook her head.

'Too late, my lady. Look!'

And sure enough, strolling down the garden towards them, beaming proudly, came Sir Francis.

'Up with the lark, my pretty,' he said, kissing Liza. 'But not arrayed for the day *we* have ahead.'

'I thought we were to visit friends, and enjoy drifting on the Thames in the new barge,' objected Liza suspiciously. 'I know I'm not dressed for *that*, but what other plans did you have in mind?'

'The *Queen's* plans, sweetness. She wants us to go to Oatlands, where she and the Court are staying at the moment. Our old friend, Hawkins, will be there, too. She is on the verge—the very verge—of deciding that we must sail and destroy the Spanish shipping before it gets a chance to destroy us. There is a new Armada, they say; a terrible fleet. The Spaniard has learned from us, and his ships are fast becoming a force to be reckoned with. So the Queen bids us go to Court before she sets off on a

Progress. Then we can leave for Plymouth, and take up our residence near where the fleet is to assemble.'

So for Liza, her lovely sunny London day was spoiled. She had to dress in her best, rigged out like the finest of the Court. Dressed in palest straw brocade, richly embroidered, with a rebato ruff, strings of priceless pearls round her throat and all the latest fads of fashion—the painted fan, an elaborate girdle, a golden, gem-encrusted billament on her head—she still regretted her quiet, ordinary day.

But if the Queen noticed the hot, resentful eyes of her master mariner's wife, she made no comment. She was at her most charming, teasing Liza for rarely coming to Court, telling Drake that with such a *dragon* to fight for her realm, she had little to fear.

They ate a light lunch with the rest of the Court, then set out at once for Plymouth, leaving Belle and the servants to pack their luggage and bring it on at a slower pace.

'What a thrilling visit to London,' grumbled Liza as they cantered into view of Plymouth, three days later. 'As for our charming house in Dowgate, I seem scarcely to have seen it since you bought it.'

'You stay in it whilst I represent Plymouth in the House of Commons and make lengthy speeches to Parliament,' objected her husband reasonably. 'When various voyages are being planned which need my assistance, though not, alas, my participation, you've lived at the Herbery with me.'

'Oh, that's not the same,' said Liza, unwilling to give up her grudge against the Queen so easily. 'It's all work then, and no chance of a little ordinary *fun.*' She eyed the town ahead, unbending a little. 'Though Plymouth is very pretty with the sun gleaming on the walls, isn't it?'

'Pretty! It's beautiful, Liza. But we'll go to Buckland as soon as I've had a look at the fleet assembling. Give us a week here and then we'll be in our country home, which I know you love as much as I do.'

'All right,' sighed Liza, unwillingly mollified. 'This latest expedition, my love. Are you sure you'll sail with it, or do you think you'll be left behind again?'

'I think I'll sail, for with me they can be sure of plenty of willing sailors—and soldiers, too—who are prepared to risk their lives, knowing I'll see them right at the end of it. But if they (or, rather, she) changes her mind, I'll steal off and climb aboard a ship, like young Essex did on that ill-fated voyage to Lisbon.'

'I believe you would,' said Liza wonderingly. 'How can you love the sea so much, Frank? It's hard work, bad living often, and always there must be danger. How can any of it be *enjoyable?*'

Rather to her surprise, Drake considered the question carefully before answering.

'It's the sense of being in *command,* of being answerable only to God for my actions,' he said quietly at length. 'It's the feeling of all those others, whose dependence is on me, and whose trust is absolute. As for danger, it's excitement I remember most. The hot rush of anger against the enemy, the boom of the cannon signalling attack.' He stopped, confused. 'I can't really explain it myself,' he finished lamely.

As they rode down High Street and turned into their own stableyard, Liza leaned across and squeezed his hand.

'You have explained it,' she said earnestly.

They spent several weeks in Plymouth, in fact, with Liza helping as best she could with the victualling of supplies for the captains. Then, at last, they went to Buckland to await final instructions.

It was pleasant there in the heat of summer. The room Sir Francis had had panelled was cool and pleasant, the panelling painted with charming scenes of the sea and the wide windows showing the most glorious views over their rolling acres. Liza often sat there, sewing, in the heat of the day, whilst her husband discussed the proposed voyage with his friends in the great hall below her.

Sometimes she walked amongst them, feeling the blessed coolness of the tiled floor sparsely strewn with rushes, but though she loved to be with her husband and his friends and act the hostess, her favourite place was definitely the withdrawing-room on the first floor.

She and Sir Francis were sitting together one evening, playing backgammon, whilst Bodenham, who acted as Drake's treasurer and book-keeper, worked at his papers in the corner, occasionally murmuring a query which Sir Francis, who kept his finger very much on the pulse of his business ventures, could generally answer without losing track of the game.

Abruptly, the door burst open. The figure of a frightened maidservant hovered in the opening for an instant, and Liza had scarcely registered that the girl's face was as white as her cap when Fenner burst into the room, red-faced and agitated.

'The Spaniards, Sir Francis,' he gasped. 'They've landed! They're burning and massacring, calling our good villagers heretics; and have punished some as such. We must ride to Plymouth at once, and see to our fortifications.'

Liza realised that she, Drake and Bodenham were all on their feet, and felt surprise that she had not noticed herself rising.

'Where, man, where?' demanded Drake fiercely. 'Not at Plymouth? Surely not at Plymouth?'

'At Mousehole, sir. They've attacked that poor fishermen's village, and burned it to the ground. Newlyn and Penzance also. I got here as quickly as I could, for the people of Plymouth are in a sorry state. We must get the fleet out, sir, and catch them still at anchorage.'

'Come, Liza,' snapped Sir Francis. His wife needed no second bidding. They were running down the stairs and out of the front door in seconds, to where the maidservant, for all her shocked face, had arranged for horses to be saddled and ready.

'That girl shall be well rewarded when we return,' said Drake, swinging somewhat heavily into the saddle. Liza jumped on to the other horse, which meant that she had to ride astride, but she was fortunately not wearing a farthingale, merely petticoats, and frequently rode astride when on their estates. As they rode off, they heard an indignant cry from Fenner, and Liza realised that the maid had provided him with a fresh horse—the one she herself had taken—leaving him no alternative now but to saddle up another beast from the stable.

As they rode hard, the smooth close-cropped grass making scarcely a sound as the horses' hooves met it, Liza realised for the first time the excitement of danger. There were Spaniards, of that she had no doubt. Captain Fenner was a man to be trusted; a steady, reliable man, not one to be taken in by a wild rumour. Yet she knew no fear as the wind tore the long strands of hair out of the gold net she was wearing, only a tremendous sense of elation. Whatever was to come, she would face it with her husband to guide her. Though she had never killed, nor thought of it, she realised now, with a drying of her mouth, that many simple Cornish people were dead, simply because no one but Sir Francis had preached danger and watchfulness. And his reward had been constant accusations both from the Queen and others of being a war-monger. One eager to stir up a battle for his own betterment.

Those that had not died by the fire would be homeless, ran her thoughts. Their boats, too, which they depended on for their livelihood, they would have been destroyed.

'Should we not make for Cornwall?' she shouted, but her small voice was carried away by the wind of their going, and Sir Francis, used to such conditions but misunderstanding her, boomed, 'Not far to go now, my love. A few minutes and we'll be riding through the town gates, if the horses don't founder.'

They rode up to the gateway, already manned to be closed as soon as danger threatened, to see faces light up as the message was passed around. 'Sir Francis, and his good lady! There can't be much danger now, or he'd not have brought young Lady Liza.'

'Go to the house, Liza,' Drake ordered peremptorily. 'Bodenham and I will make for Sutton Pool. The fleet must be alerted and moved into the Sound. But I fear we shall be too late.'

And when he returned, late that night, it was to tell Liza that the Spaniards had landed, done their cruel work, and sailed quickly off again, whilst the contrary wind would have made getting out of the Sound difficult, in any case.

'I would like to kill every one of them,' Liza said in a small, tight voice. 'What have we done to them to deserve such treatment? You've taken towns and destroyed them, shipping has been lost in mutual fighting, but I've heard you boast many a time that not an enemy life was lost amongst the innocent Spanish townspeople.'

'I'm not a Spanish fanatic, crying, "I do this for the Catholic faith", to fool myself that Christ watches with approval,' Drake said bitterly. 'Well, Liza, the people of Plymouth are safe enough. The Spanish fleet have gone too far along the coast to attack us now, and, anyway, we're well fortified and a watch is always kept. But we'll stay in Plymouth, sweetheart, until the fleet sails. It will be good for morale for everyone to know that my wife, the person I prize more than any other living being, is in Plymouth. The men will know their own women are safe, and will thus be able to give their whole minds to getting the fleet prepared.'

'I like to be near you, and now you must be near the ships,' Liza assured him.

★ ★ ★ ★

Yet when they did sail, it was almost as a favour from the Queen. As a result of the raid on Cornwall, she tried to insist that the fleet first sail around the coast of Ireland—for a rebellion was brewing, as usual, on that most troublesome island—then they must sail along the coast of Spain to make sure a huge invasion fleet was not being prepared in some hidden harbour. In addition, they must pledge their words to be back in

England by May, 1596.

'It's utterly impossible, and they all know it, the lick-spittle hypocrites,' snarled Drake, and Liza knew how he must feel to let such harsh words escape his lips. 'Does she *want* every port from the Lizard to the Humber to feel the flames of the Inquisition before she makes a move? We have soldiers on board, and when large numbers of men are herded together in ships, there breeds plague and infection. To do as she asks would be to lose our fighting men and probably half our crews without a blow exchanged. A fine way to attack and destroy Panama, let alone have enough men left to seize Spanish treasure and make our way back to England with it! Then she presents us with a date by which we must have returned from our voyage, when every sailor knows there is only One who can ordain the time of our return.'

'You'd better not be so outspoken to the Queen,' advised Liza. 'Do find a tactful way of saying it, my darling.'

But then news came in from a reliable spy in Spain that the *Capitana,* the biggest ship of the Mexican treasure fleet, had been dismasted and was repairing the damage in Puerto Rico harbour—with her bounty of two and a half million in gold and silver unguarded, for she had missed her escort of fighting ships.

The Queen promptly changed her mind yet again. Now they were to set sail at once for Puerto Rico, capture the treasure ship and then continue on their way to Panama.

So Liza arranged for their friends to come to a farewell party, and William Courtenay came with his tilted smile and satirical glances.

'I'm almost tempted to join this venture,' he said to Liza in a low voice. 'But why is Sir John Hawkins sharing your husband's command? He's old and tired. He's been a bold enough man in his time, but he has reached the years when a man doesn't take a decision without long and careful thought. Drake isn't like that now—unless he's changed in the last few months—so why try to harness the slow old carthorse and the lively warhorse to one plough? They'll rub against each other like two itching sores.'

Liza laughed, but even to her own ears the sound was hollow. 'Sir John *is* old; one would take him for more than sixty-three,' she admitted. 'But I think the Queen feels

Sir Francis is too daring, and Sir John is too careful, and they will balance each other, so to speak.'

'What rubbish,' drawled Courtenay contemptuously. 'They'll never pull together as a team, yet neither will give in willingly to the other. They'll bicker and fight and the venture will fail. No, I'd not put a penny into *this* expedition.'

'The venture is well backed already,' snapped Liza, moving away from her tormentor to talk with other guests. But he had only voiced aloud her own doubts. Already Hawkins and Drake had shown signs of disagreement, and there seemed to be a mutual antipathy developing in them which had never shown before this joint command.

Well at least, she comforted herself, if this voyage is another failure, he'll give up the sea. I'll wave him off tomorrow and pray with every heartbeat that they meet with success, but should they fail, what will we lose? A little pride will be hurt, of course, but he'll realise he's too old for these voyages. He'll stay at home, enjoy his wealth and property, and perhaps—who knows?—I might bear him a son.

★ ★ ★ ★

The ships returned before May, despite Drake's openly expressed doubts. They had met with no success, they had brought back with them no treasure, only tales of dismaying failure. The only bright spark seemed to be that the weary fleet, limping homeward, did meet the newest Spanish Armada and beat them back despite being by far the smaller and weaker force.

So much and more did Baskerville tell the Lady Elizabeth Drake, standing awkwardly in her warm parlour where she had spread out a welcoming feast for her husband and his shipmates.

'Will they be long?' she asked, at length. She had been married to a sailor for too many years to expect that he would rush to her side before he had seen to his men and his ships.

'Sir John Hawkins is dead,' Baskerville told her. William Whitlocke, a handsome young man who had sailed as Drake's body servant (the coveted post held once by Isabelle's first husband) hovered. He was fair-haired and of an almost girlish prettiness. Yet he, too, seemed strangely ill at ease.

But at last he stepped forward and said, 'Drake is dead, Lady Liza. We buried his body at sea.'

She could only stare. It was, she knew, completely impossible. Drake could not die—simply succumb—as other men could. They must be raving.

Other men came with the same story, and received the same blank, disbelieving look from wide, dark eyes. Always she asked so politely of each new arrival, 'Will he be long?'

Belle was summoned, and she sat her mistress in a comfortable chair and gestured the men away. She had to repeat over and over, for what seemed like hours, that Drake would never come home again. That he was dead. Dead, as others he loved were dead. As her cousin Geoffrey was dead.

It took Belle a long time to get her mistress to bed that night. Liza kept fixing her with wide, incredulous eyes and saying, 'Dead? My Frank, really dead?' And Belle would assure her, tears slipping unheeded down her tired face, that Drake would never cross the Hoe again, save in spirit. As she settled Liza for the night, she heard Liza's voice, low and droning, like a child

learning its lesson, saying over and over,
'He's dead, he's dead.'

* * * *

During the weeks that followed, Liza heard
the story of the tragic, yet in some way
inevitable, voyage in snatches. Some parts
of it were told straightforwardly enough,
others were whispered. But in the end she
pieced together most of the tale.

It had begun with the joint commanders
disagreeing within days of leaving Plymouth. Drake, in the light of previous
experience, wanted to attack the Canaries,
for ransom, loot, and morale boosting,
besides, of course, the revictualling which
was a necessity before crossing the Atlantic.

Sir John Hawkins immediately opposed
the idea, and bitter arguing turned to
plain open dislike and mutual dismay at
their shared commission. Baskerville, with
tremendous tact, had persuaded Hawkins
to agree, and Hawkins grudgingly did
so, probably, thought Liza, because he
guessed that if he refused Drake would
attack without him!

They sailed, therefore, to attack Las
Palmas, but lingered too long in choosing

a landing place. The Spaniards, forewarned by the tardiness shown by the Queen, had manned their ports strongly this time. Drake had taught them a lesson he was now to regret. Everywhere he went it seemed, desperate Spaniards awaited him and instead of neglected defences and a 'come day, go day' attitude, he found fortifications, strongly manned defences, and vigilance.

So Las Palmas went unmolested, and the fleet watered at an uninhabited bay. A bad beginning, as everyone realised.

Things worsened when the Spanish captured the *Francis*. Five of their treasure ships had seen the two small English vessels lagging behind the main body of the fleet and had seized the *Francis*, though her sister ship, the *Delight*, managed to escape. Her captain immediately went to Drake's flagship, the *Defiance*, and told of the disaster. Drake was horrified and wanted to chase after the treasure fleet and the captured English ship, knowing that otherwise all their plans would be common knowledge to every Spaniard from end to end of their empire. But Hawkins stuck his toes in. Like a bulldog who has grabbed his victim and will not let go, whatever the cost, Hawkins insisted that they must waste no more time. They must go on.

'Hawkins was already ill,' Baskerville explained. 'Young Clifford—you remember him, milady?—was of the opinion that we should press on. I'm a soldier, and know little of sea strategy. Yet it seemed to me that had we chased the Spaniards and captured them, even if we had cut only one from the fleet and stopped the others from returning to Puerto Rico, we'd have restored morale by gaining a very rich prize and been able to surprise the Spanish. But Drake did not press his old friend. He must have had some foreknowledge then, for I've never known him to allow a decision to go against him with less fuss. And accordingly, we made for Puerto Rico.'

'Were you not stopped on the way? Did no fleet set out to intercept you?' asked Liza.

'No, for whilst we prepared ourselves for action and took aboard fresh water at the Virgin Islands your husband got out his charts and found a new route to Puerto Rico. He succeeded splendidly in the surprise, therefore. But though they could not understand how we had managed to escape their other traps, they were well prepared. The treasure fleet was home and safe and the warning delivered.

'The harbour was well defended. Impossible to attack, by sea. But there was a spot, which the Spaniards thought too hazardous for us to attack, so rocky and dangerous it was. But we attacked. Without success.'

Liza did not question him further. She knew of the terrible loss of life which had resulted from a daring night attack under the guns of the defenders. Drake had hoped to get so near before discovery, she believed, that the forts would have mainly shot over their heads. Instead they were spotted early, and the deadliest fire crashed into the small boats and pinnaces, causing such havoc that threats had to be used to make the living take the oars of the dead, to row them back to the ships.

'Sir Francis tried to attack the harbour, hoping to slip round the boom which guarded it,' Baskerville went on. 'It was a masterly piece of seamanship, to see him bring those craft swooping like birds upon the harbour mouth. But the Spanish fellow in charge sunk two fully laden merchant ships, a *capitana* and another frigate, so that there was no passageway in or out.

'Hawkins had died during the run down to Puerto Rico. Now, Drake was in sole command. He decided we would leave that place and make for Nombre de Dios. On the way we seized Rio de la Hacha, and got a good haul in hidden treasure and pearls. It heartened the men—those that were left had felt not only grief over Sir John's death, but that misfortune lay heavy upon the venture.'

'So it did,' Liza said drearily, and Baskerville could only nod in sympathetic agreement.

'We met little resistance in Nombre de Dios, for they had been warned by the people of Rio de la Hacha. I set off in command of seven hundred and fifty men or so. We marched, of course, on Panama. But we never got near it. The weather was terrible and the rain ruined our powder so we could scarcely fire our pieces. The line chosen as easiest and best was closely guarded by Spanish troops.

'We were gone four days. When we got back to Nombre de Dios it seemed as though our lack of success killed the hope that had never, until then, left Drake. He had to force himself to smile in front of the men, but the jokes rang hollow, leaving a sour taste on the tongue. I think all of us in some position of command knew that with the loss of absolute faith in his own power to win through, your husband was badly handicapped. It had brought him through impossible situations in the past. Now it had gone. He no longer *believed* in himself.'

'The end?' said Liza at last, her voice small and remote.

'Dysentery. It flew through the ships like wildfire, and when it struck Drake, it struck a man already broken of heart. He lacked the *desire* for life. He died, delirious, and we laid out his body and sailed into Puerto Bello. The settlement there was to take the place of Puerto Rico, thought—with reason—to be an unhealthy spot. We burned it to the ground for his funeral pyre, Lady Liza.

'Then I sailed a league out to sea, and his body, in a lead coffin, and the prizes he had taken, together with two of his ships, were sunk. We knew what manner of man we buried that day. He could have succeeded, had we been given even half the information we needed. Had he been allowed to go to sea earlier, and quietly reconnoitre in Spanish waters, he would have seen for himself how his earlier actions had woken the Spaniard to a sense of his own danger. But it was not to be. I know all his friends, living and dead, would agree that we have lost the greatest seaman, the greatest strategist and the bravest man this age has known.'

Liza inclined her head in thanks, and said briefly, 'Clifford was killed, was he not? And Brute Brown, who must have been one of my husband's closest friends. Poor Nick Clifford! It was said that he went on this expedition because the Queen was horrid to him—how much more horrid was fate.'

'How was she horrid to Nick?' asked Baskerville, trying not to sound amused. What a reason for going to sea—that the Queen had been 'horrid'!

'Oh, he fought with you in France, did he not? And the French King Henry IV gave him a decoration of some sort for gallantry. Poor young Clifford was proud of it, and wore it at Court. My husband told me that, in front of all the Court, the Queen roared, "Clifford, go and take that—that *thing* off. Learn, you foolish puppy, that *my* dogs wear *my* collars." '

'Poor Clifford, no wonder he wanted to win some renown in an English battle,' said Baskerville. 'But death comes to us all, my lady.'

She agreed, but absently.

Long after Baskerville had left, she added the bits and sketches of the voyage she had learned from other sources. Her husband had died raving mad, some said. All agreed that he had said such things in his delirium that no man would, for Drake's own sake, repeat. Many people blamed the failure to destroy Panama on his eagerness to attack Rio de la Hacha, and said it was revenge, because he had suffered his first setback there, years earlier. They said that Hawkins had written such things in his will about Drake that she must never be allowed to hear them. Whispered words hinted that they were true words Hawkins had penned.

How much of it, she wondered, lay at my door? How much or how little did I really understand him, and help him when he needed help? I was a good wife, a good hostess to his friends. But how much did my resentment hurt him, because he came to my bed for sleep and not for lovemaking?

She was to wonder this for many sleepless nights, and even her conclusion gave her little comfort. For she decided she had made not one jot of difference. His home life was so divorced from his life at sea that even had they been at each other's throats it would not have affected his outlook once he was at sea again. Even at home, she doubted whether he had worried overmuch about his lack of interest in her as a bedpartner.

Which was worse, she wondered idly, as she lay in her lonely bed? To believe your viewpoint and feelings had adversely affected your husband, or to know in your heart that most of the time he had not noticed your slight coolness, your lack of enthusiasm, and your longing for the child he could not give you?

There was no answer. She could only remember him constantly as he had first been; her kind and gentle lover who always put her wishes and desires before his own.

And I'll have many years to remember him, she thought, for I'm only twenty-nine. I'm a rich widow, so my bed will probably not be empty for long. As for my heart, I wonder if there's a man alive who could awaken it, and bring back the warmth and gaiety that I had in our early married years.

13

REMARRIAGE

'You'll have to make up your mind whether you will take Sir William Courtenay or not, Lady Liza,' Belle told her mistress roundly as the constant squabbles and bickering over Drake's will began to get on both their nerves. 'He's always had a fancy for you, and—it's no use denying it—you've always had a soft spot for him. Sir Francis is dead and will never return; you are taking nothing from him by remarrying. Indeed, he often used to say before a voyage that he hoped in the event of his death you *would* remarry.'

'How do you know he's asked me to marry him?' Liza said, smiling up at Belle in the mirror.

Belle shrugged, plying the brush so vigorously on the thick black hair that Liza winced.

'Courtenay doesn't waste his time riding over to see how you get on just for the sake of his health,' she said blightingly. 'He's been very patient with you, milady, he's respected your grief. But he's waited long enough. Are you going to marry him or aren't you?'

'If you pull every hair on my head out by the roots I'm likely to remain a widow till I die, like it or not,' she said. 'Besides, I'm a rich woman now, Belle. Father died two years ago and Mother was in her grave two years before that. I've inherited all his lands and property, and now I've Buckland and many other manors left me by my husband. The mills are mine, and they make a huge profit, as I'm sure you know. Why should I drop into Sir William's hands like a ripe peach, as though he were my only hope of remarriage? I'm very sure if I went back to Court I'd not lack admirers, even if their main eye was to my property rather than my person.'

Belle began coiling and pinning the heavy masses of hair into as small a knot as she could manage. She fitted on the black velvet hood, and looked fondly at Liza's reflection.

'A prettier face would be hard to find,' she said honestly. 'Nor a prettier figure.

Why, Lady Liza, do you think Sir William has waited so long for your money? He could have married a rich widow any time, for they are always chasing after him. You're not yet thirty, and perhaps because you've borne no children you look younger. I've always thought that in your heart you had more than a simple liking for Sir William. If it's true, then why not tell him so, and marry?'

'He's so different from Sir Francis,' muttered Liza, bending her head so that Belle would not see how her cheeks burned at the thought of marriage to Courtenay. 'He's not gentle, or thoughtful, you know, Belle. He's selfish and arrogant, and though he's not remarried, that hasn't stopped him from having a woman in his bed. Suppose we *did* marry? How long do you think it would take him to tire of me and begin to lie with the maidservants again?'

'That would depend on you, my lady,' said Belle with unaccustomed severity. 'He only broke loose from his first wife because she kept him on too tight a rein. She was sharp, and spiteful. She never laughed with him, or went hunting with him, or made any attempt to be anything but a bedpartner and a watcher. You would, I trust, be different.'

'She was always pregnant,' reminded Liza. 'Seven live children in nine years, and three dead ones. That isn't much of a life for any woman.'

'But you'd love to have a child ...' began Belle, when Liza cut in, laughing.

'A child, yes. Not a child every nine months. But you're right, Belle. I'll speak to Sir William. He's coming to see me today, and a relief it will be to see a smiling face instead of my horrible brother-in-law's mean mouth and narrowed eyes, and all the others flocking round trying to persuade me to interfere in Sir Francis' will, which interests me not at all.'

So when Courtenay called for her later in the day, to take her walking or riding, whichever she preferred, she chose a walk in the pleasure gardens.

'The apples are ripe,' remarked Sir William. 'A sure sign that autumn is on the way, my dear. Have you made your plans for keeping them in store during the winter months?'

Liza looked up at him. His mocking gaze held hers, and he said softly, 'No, Liza. I'm not going to ask you again. Next time, *you* must ask *me.*'

'Ask you what? How best to store apples?' said Liza quickly, but though he laughed, she knew he had noticed and appreciated the colour that had flooded her face.

'You have a bailiff to advise you on estate matters. And a good agent to advise you on how much you should store for the winter, and how much you should sell. But never forget, Liza, winter is usually with us sooner than we think.'

Liza took a deep breath and looked Sir William straight in the eye. 'In that case, it would be best if I accepted your offer without further ado. Your offer of *marriage*, I mean,' she amended carefully. 'I don't think that your children would resent my presence, but I've no doubt you would like to tell them the happy news yourself. Then by the time I have made my arrangements here, and the knot is tied, your offspring will have grown used to the idea of having a stepmother.'

A shout of laughter was surprised from him. Then, in the tawny grass of the orchard with only the trees to watch, he held her close and kissed her mouth—a long, sensual kiss which made Liza shudder as she stood within his arms.

Releasing her, he said teasingly, 'How shall I wait for the day I make you mine?'

And Liza, laughing and breathless, thought to herself: How shall *I* wait, who have never known the embraces of a lustful man?

★ ★ ★ ★

'There, milady, you look a very fine bride indeed,' said Belle approvingly.

The two women had talked long and hard over this wedding day. Should she, as a widow, wear her hair loose? Should she don the gown which she longed to wear—primrose satin sewn with pearls and emeralds? Or would it look unbecoming on one of her years?

But now the moment had come, and she was to be escorted to the church by her uncle. It no longer seemed to matter what anyone thought. Only William Courtenay.

★ ★ ★ ★

'Nice—to be going to bed with a woman one has known for fifteen years, and loved for fifteen years,' remarked William conversationally as they entered their nuptial chamber after the wedding guests had been sent on their way.

'What about all the others you've bedded between those sheets?' said Liza forthrightly. 'Didn't you love any of the procession of Molls, and Dolls, and Biddys, and Peggys?'

'I've had the sheets changed!' William told her. 'I may be a widower, but I know better than to bring a bride home to used sheets. These smell of lavender and fresh air. Come along, hurry yourself out of your shift, girl. I can't wait to see you without all the frills and fopperies of clothing.'

He stood and smiled with a certain bewilderment at her sudden shyness, then untied the draw-string round her neck and pulled the garment off her body himself. Now they both stood naked, and she looked up at him frankly, her dark eyes unashamed.

'Well?'

'Oh, well indeed. Very, very well. Liza, you're ripe for the taking. Get into bed before I disgrace myself by jumping at you on the floor. Don't giggle, girl, this is a serious moment in our lives. By God, but I seem to have waited for this moment all my life. You fit as close to my side as a nut in its shell. Presently we'll be closer still.'

They climbed into bed and Liza felt the quickening of every pulse in her body, hammering out her feelings of fear, anticipation and excitement, as they had not done for many years.

'My only love,' murmured Courtenay, and even as their passion mounted she had time for a flicker of amusement over forgotten Molls, Polls and Biddys. Then she was carried on the tide of their love, over the mountain and up, up into the singing heights.

★ ★ ★ ★

During the days that followed, Liza found herself slipping easily and happily into the life of her new home. She loved her stepchildren and they loved her; the servants, at first inclined to be supercilious with a mistress so young, soon found her to be capable of dealing with the most recalcitrant. As for Courtenay, she soon realised that her early diagnosis of his character had been correct.

He was not gentle, or thoughtful, towards his wife. But he loved her, and he appreciated her tactful handling of the servants and his children. Occasionally, she found his demands on her body exhausting, but she never protested. She remembered Isabelle's words of wisdom on how the first Lady Elizabeth Courtenay had lost her husband's affections, and she was determined not to do likewise.

Then she found, to her delighted amazement, that she was pregnant. Sir William, already a father, showed a pleasure that she found touching. He was careful of her now, less abrupt if she begged to be excused from a hunting party, or a game of shooting the longbow.

Rather alarming to her were the sessions of retching and straining over a basin, which left her weak and listless. But her eldest stepdaughter, Margaret, told her with a motherly air that it was often so; first babies brought bad morning sickness which had to be endured, sometimes until the fifth month.

'Then the baby moves, and the sickness seems to go away,' she told Liza comfortingly. 'And often, a woman who suffers as you have with her first, has little or no trouble with her other pregnancies.'

Liza, still white-faced and shaky limbed

from the last violent bout of breakfast-losing, said huskily, 'Other pregnancies? Good God, girl, I'm beginning to think a first baby is one too many.'

'You'll feel differently when he moves, so they say,' Margaret said briskly. 'You will tell me when he starts to stir, won't you, Lady Liza?'

'If I live through it,' said Liza gloomily, bending over the basin again.

In spite of her youth, Margaret proved a good judge of the behaviour of a baby in the womb. One morning Liza woke feeling fresh and pleasant. She got cautiously out of bed, waiting for the hot dizziness and the swimming head as she drew herself upright. Nothing happened. A cautious tour of the bedroom, and she still felt fine. Rose helped her to dress, and she broke her fast cautiously but with more pleasure than she had for some weeks.

A day or two later, she felt the tiny fin-fluttering that is a baby's first movement. Wild with excitement, she described the feeling over and over, eager for the next performance of such an extraordinary sensation.

But though the great event of her life was beginning to loom larger, she still kept firmly to her self-imposed duties of educating the young Courtenays. Then one day the baby's movements were clear enough for Rose, dressing her, to see.

'Oh, milady, did you feel the child leap? I saw an elbow—or was it a knee?—rear up and travel across your belly. All those years married, Lady Liza, and yet you quickened as soon as Sir William gets you in his bed.'

'Sir Francis was a wonderful man. A great man, Rose. It was his eternal sadness that he could father no children, and the country's eternal loss. He made me very happy, the only sadness in my life was that I bore no children. Now I have a child within my womb and perhaps that will satisfy my female vanity, or even my motherly instincts. But, Rose, it detracts not one jot from Sir Francis' greatness, both as a private and a public figure, that he could not get me with child. And Sir William, after all, has done no more than the simplest mariner in the fleet probably could.'

Rose smiled and agreed, but Liza doubted whether she had really understood what had been said.

Oddly enough, it was Courtenay himself

who seemed to share her feelings most over the baby.

'You would have liked a child by Sir Francis, for his sake and for the sake of the child,' he said one night, in a rare moment of tenderness. 'But perhaps, though he could not plant a baby in your womb, the very fact that you were his wife for eleven years has left a trace of greatness within you. This child may well bear the trace of that greatness.'

Liza truly loved him then, for understanding how she could be delighted over the coming of the baby, yet saddened because it seemed to show Sir Francis as incapable of giving her the ultimate joy.

★ ★ ★ ★

She was sitting in the garden with Margaret, enjoying the buds of May which scented the air, and the green mist of young leaves on the trees, when she first felt discomfort.

She shifted her position on the chair, trying to move the cushions round to the ache in her back.

'What's the matter, Lady Liza?'

'I don't know, Meg, my dear. The baby

isn't moving, but I have a pain. No, not a pain really. I just feel uncomfortable and as if this chair is the wrong shape or something.'

'Let's stroll down to the estuary,' suggested Margaret. 'Perhaps you've sat too long, and have a touch of cramp.'

But they did not reach the estuary. Half-way there, Margaret looked at her stepmother's ashen face, with the sweat pouring down it, and said, 'We'd better get you into bed, Lady Liza. I think the baby's coming.'

'It's too early,' moaned Liza. She was still moaning. 'Too early, too soon,' as the nurse undressed her and propped her up in bed, telling her that when she felt the urge to push, she was to pull on the sheet knotted to the bedpost.

The midwife arrived, Courtenay hovered at the door, Meg's anxious young face kept sliding in and out of Liza's range of vision. Yet still the baby did not come.

Pain had become a part of her, Liza thought, as Margaret wiped her face with a damp cloth and the midwife massaged her back. Pain was wrenching and tearing at her body and her panic-stricken mind was full of pain, too.

Because the baby was coming early—much too early. She could not bear to lose this child, who had been a part of her for so long. She must fight the pain, and do as the midwife told her, for the child's sake. But it was all so difficult. Voices echoed hollowly round and round in her head, making a senseless sound. Faces swam into view, distorted by pain and sweat so that they were scarcely recognisable.

Later—it seemed like years later—her body lay at peace, delivered of its burden. Courtenay sat beside her and tried to hold her hands, but fever burned, and she turned and cried out for 'Frank, Frank,' so that Margaret ran, sobbing, from the room and the women in attendance turned embarrassed eyes away from their master.

After a night made hideous by fevered dreams, Liza woke at dawn knowing who she was and eager to hear of the child.

'You had a fine boy, my dear. He's been washed and pronounced perfect. When you're stronger you shall see him,' Sir William told her gently.

She did not argue, but lay back on the pillows. Her face, yellowed by pain and fever, seemed more beautiful than ever as a tiny smile touched her lips.

'Frank always wanted a boy.'

He had to bend close to hear the words. He glanced, panic-filled, at the women. They could only shrug and tend the Lady Liza with helpless pity. She was very ill, but she was young and strong.

'Hope and prayer are our only weapons now,' the midwife whispered to him at midnight. Now it seemed that it was going to be enough.

With a tremendous effort, Liza opened her eyes. She gazed at Courtenay in the dancing sunlight and said faintly, 'I must see him. Bring candles; I shall not be able to see him without, for it is still so dark.'

Courtenay stumbled across the sunny room, his eyes so blurred with tears that he almost missed the bundle the midwife was holding out to him.

He hurried back to the bed and held the swaddled child close to his wife. She tried to raise herself and failed, then gazed intently at the tiny face.

'He's the image, the very image of my ...' Her voice trailed into silence and her head fell untidily on to the pillows.

Courtenay almost threw the bundle into the midwife's arms as he tried to rouse

Liza, knowing as he did so that his was a hopeless task. She had gone beyond his reach now, she was with Frank now—and she knew of his deception.

But looking on her face, calm in death, he could not believe she would hold it against him. The baby she had borne had never sucked air into its tiny lungs, never breathed or opened its puffed eyelids. It was as though it had never existed.

Yet he had made her last few moments of life happier with a small lie—that the baby at least was alive and normal. He looked down at the small, bluish face in the folds of the shawl the midwife had huddled round its tiny, lifeless body. Slowly, he bent over the bed and moved Liza's arm away from her side. She cradled her dead child as naturally as though she knew what she was holding.

Courtenay straightened her head on the pillow and tried, clumsily, to tidy her hair. The children would have to see her, and he wanted them to remember Liza as beautiful, not a thing to be feared; a dead body lolling in a great bed, which would give them nightmares.

When he had finished his self-appointed task he moved towards the door, and then turned and looked back for a moment.

'You had it all, you lucky devil, Drake,' he murmured, a half-smile on his lips. 'You had her true love, you had her admiration for your greatness, you had fame and riches. And at the last, dammit, I believe she credited you with giving her a son.'

He left the room and, with his presence missing, the women began to bustle round, setting the place to rights.

Margaret crept in, unnoticed, and knelt by the bed. She stroked Liza's cold hand, and timidly touched the baby's icy, petal-soft cheek.

'You've got all you really wanted now, Lady Liza,' she murmured to the still figure on the bed. 'You had to die to get it, my best of mothers, but you've got your *real* husband back now, and you've taken him the baby he wanted.' She crept out of the room again, pausing, as her father had done, for one last glance.

'We were just an interlude,' she murmured, as she closed the door behind her.

This Large Print Book for the Partially sighted, who cannot read normal print, is published under the auspices of

THE ULVERSCROFT FOUNDATION